Outback Dust:
The Drifter

ANNIE SEATON

The Augathella Girls: Book 7

ANNIE SEATON

ISBN 978-0-6457010-6-7

THE AUGATHELLA GIRLS

Book 1: Outback Roads –The Nanny
Book 2: Outback Sky – The Pilot
Book 3: Outback Escape – The Sister
Book 4: Outback Winds – The Jillaroo
Book 5: Outback Dawn – The Visitor
Book 6: Outback Moonlight – The Rogue
Book 7: Outback Dust – The Drifter
Book 8: Outback Hope – The Farmer

Augathella Characters - Book 7

Bec Hunter	Nurse
Matt Randall	Singer/Barman
Jacinta Mason	Teacher
Ryan Francesco	Jacinta's partner
Harry Higgins	Local doctor
Laura Adnum	Temporary midwife
Braden and Callie Cartwright	*Kilcoy Station*
Rory, Nigel and Petie	Braden's sons from his previous marriage
Kent and Sophie Mason	*Lara Waters*
Jon and Fallon Ingram	Station managers
Ben Riley and Amelia Foley	Shire engineer & station hand
Tom and Jenny Riley	Ben's parents
Kimberley Riordan	Deputy principal
Quinn Calthorpe	*Merry Downs Station*
Old Reg	Local character

Chapter 1

Kent and Sophie

'Happy, Mrs Mason?' Sophie's husband of three and a half hours leaned over and kissed her cheek. 'Ready to dance with me?'

'Very, Mr Mason. And I am.' Sophie smiled as Kent took her hand and drew her to her feet. She was so happy, her cheeks were aching from the constant wide smile. Her husband waited patiently as she adjusted the voluminous skirt of her wedding dress. Her smile grew even wider; she could now refer to Kent as her husband. When they had been waiting at the door of the church before the ceremony, Braden had told her she looked like a big ball of white fairy floss, but Sophie knew, from her big brother, that was a compliment. Braden might be an excellent cattleman, but he wasn't the best with words, although Callie, his wife of three months had been working on him, and he was much more open these days. Sophie smiled again as Rory, Nigel and Petie tore across the dance floor and headed outside.

Craig Wilson was the MC for the reception and he'd just tapped on the microphone and called the bride and groom up for the bridal waltz. Sophie was looking forward to the dance. She and Kent had been practising the waltz every night for the past two months and she knew they had it down pat. The nerves that had been with her until the moment she'd seen Kent waiting for her at the altar had long disappeared, and they had simply enjoyed the celebration of their wedding with their family and friends.

Braden caught her eye as Sophie and Kent walked behind the bridal table; his smile was slow and sweet. Callie turned and Sophie touched her gently on the shoulder. Her sister-in-law's eyes were full of happiness.

Her nephews had done them proud, Petie had been the ring bearer, and Rory and Nigel had acted as ushers. Craig, the MC, was in the middle of an anecdote so Sophie stopped at the end of the table, and Kent's arm went around her waist as she spoke to her brother and his wife.

'I can't wait to see the photos of the boys. They look gorgeous.'

'Almost outdid the groom,' Kent said with a grin.

'Almost outdid their father.' Callie laughed. 'We had to queue to get in the bathroom. Rory was putting gel in Petie's hair to make it stand up.'

'He did good. It looked great,' Sophie said.

'After I combed it out.' Braden chuckled.

'Where were they heading when they ran across the floor?' Sophie asked. 'Are they worried they're going to get roped into dancing?'

'No, I said they could go out and run for a while before it gets dark.' Braden reached for his beer glass.

'They've been really good,' Callie said. 'They've had a ball. Nigel said it was the best wedding he's ever been to, and then he and Rory had their first blue when Rory told him it was the first one he'd been to.'

'Go dance, you pair,' Braden said. 'The singer guy is hanging onto the mike ready to start. He's got a great voice. Where did you find him?'

'Matt's a friend of Bec and Jacinta's. They first heard him up at Tambo pub. He's brilliant, isn't he?'

'He's fantastic. I thought it was a Jack Johnson CD playing when he first started singing,' Callie said.

'Mr and Mrs Mason, please take the dance floor,' Craig called over the microphone.

Kent led Sophie onto the dance floor and a wave of happiness surged through her as he pulled her close. Their wedding day had been perfect; despite the forecast of strong winds and dust storms, the sky had stayed a brilliant clear summer blue, with not a breath of wind. The ceremony had been emotional, and as tears had filled Kent's eyes when he had taken her hands from Braden's, Sophie knew their lifetime of happiness was about to begin.

After the nuptials, they'd stepped out through the front door of the Anglican church building onto the lush lawn and into a shower of rose petals. Amelia, Bec, and Jacinta had raced out the back door of the church and picked up the baskets of petals picked from Jenny Riley's garden early that morning. The fragrance of the roses had been beautiful and Sophie knew the memory would stay with her for the rest of her life.

Everyone she loved was there to celebrate with them, and her eyes filled when she glanced across at the memorial plaque to her parents at the side of the church. The crowd of guests had gathered on the lawn, and many locals waved from outside the fence as she and Kent made slow progress on their way towards the bridal cars. It was a full hour before the bridal party headed out to the river with the photographer.

The catering had been done by the CWA ladies under the supervision of Kent's mum. She'd been president before they'd moved to Brisbane because of his dad's health issues. The roast dinner had been beautifully presented, and the variety of homemade desserts had been decadent. The cake which took pride of place on a high table beside the bridal table was going to be cut immediately after the waltz.

'It's been a perfect day, hasn't it, Soph?' Kent whispered in her ear as the soft, slow notes of their chosen song filled the air.

'It has. A fitting start to our life together.' Sophie reached up and brushed her lips over Kent's as the vocalist began to sing. 'Now I'm looking forward to having you all to myself for the next ten days.'

'No cattle, no early morning calls, just tropical beaches, cocktails and lots of sleeping in,' Kent said.

'The sleeping in bit sounds good to me. Fiji, here we come.' Sophie closed her eyes and rested her head on her husband's shoulder as the music surrounded her.

Chapter 2

Callie and Braden

'Sophie told me that as soon as Kent's mum and dad join them we have to dance too.' Braden pulled nervously at his bowtie as she watched. 'Are you ready, Cal?'

'I am. Are you?'

'As ready as I'll ever be, love. At least they're all watching Sophie and Kent and won't notice my two left feet.'

'You've done well. Just remember what I taught you. Sophie looks beautiful, doesn't she? And so happy.'

'It's great to see that haunted look in her eyes finally gone. She had a tough few years.' Braden's eyes were full of happiness as he watched his sister dance with her husband.

'You all did,' Callie said quietly. 'Come on, hop up. Kent's parents are on the floor now. It's our turn.'

Braden stood and Callie followed him to the dance floor. She loved this man with her heart and soul. He opened his arms and she stepped into them.

'One, two, three,' he said quietly against her cheek as he led her into the waltz. He stopped counting and Callie smiled as his natural rhythm took over. Her husband was a much better dancer than he gave himself credit for.

'We've turned a corner and now everything's going to be fine. A new beginning for all of us,' he said as he focused on his steps. 'We're all happy. Finally. Even Nige is back to normal.'

A shiver ran down Callie's back. 'Don't tempt fate, Braden. Let's just live in the moment and enjoy the happiness we have every day.'

'We owe it all to you, you know, my love. That sassy nanny who broke down on our red dust road and almost had her designer luggage washed away in the irrigation channel has changed our lives.' Braden's arms pulled her closer. 'You look beautiful tonight, Callie. It's not just the makeup and the fancy dress. You're glowing with happiness. You look sort of different.'

Callie hesitated. Maybe it was the right time to tell Braden her news. *Their* news.

'I am happy. This is Sophie's day, but you're right. I am different.'

'Because you're happier?'

'I'm always happy. You and the three boys make me happy every moment of every day.'

'Every moment?' Braden grinned down at her.

'Well, maybe not when Petie won't eat his veggies, and when Nigel has the occasional tantrum, but I can deal with that.'

'*We* can. A little bit of discipline goes a long way. They're good kids.'

'I wasn't going to tell you why I'm extra happy, but Sophie guessed when we were getting ready because I wouldn't have a glass of champagne. At least she asked, but I didn't tell her. I wanted you to be the first to know, Braden.'

A sudden gust of wind rippled the sides of the marquee as Braden held her gaze. Callie blinked away happy tears. Her husband came to a stop in the middle of the dance floor and stared down at her. 'The first to know? Know what? Is everything okay?'

'More than okay. Wonderful, in fact. You're going to be a dad again.' Callie's last words caught on a breath as Braden's mouth lifted in a huge grin.

'I'm going to be a dad again? You're having a baby?'

'Yes, *we're* having a baby. And I'm scared. It's all new to me.'

'Oh, my love, what a perfect day. Let's go and tell the boys.'

Callie chuckled. 'I think we need to finish the dance first. We'll go get them after this song. It's time they came inside, and the cake will be cut soon.'

Braden let go of her and put his hands on either side of her face. 'Have I told you today how much I love you, Callie?'

'You have, but I never tire of hearing it.'

'I love you to the moon and back, Callie Cartwright.'

Chapter 3

Jacinta and Ryder

'Show us your moves, baby.'

Jacinta Mason giggled as Ryder tugged her hands and pulled her out onto the dance floor. The family was all up on the floor waltzing, and now Kent and Sophie's friends were joining the bridal waltz.

'You show me *your* moves, Mr Dancer Boy.'

'Ooh.' Ryder's low voice sent warm tingles running through Jacinta. 'I'll show you my moves, but a little bit later. I've got a bottle of Moet chilling in our room.'

'Our room? What room?'

'My room at the hotel tonight. I wanted it to be a totally special night. Your bedroom combined study is a bit off-putting for romance. I've booked the suite.'

'Romance?' Jacinta widened her smile as Ryder took her into his arms and the tempo of the music increased. 'I haven't packed my PJs.'

'No matter, you won't be needing them.'

'Cheeky.' Jacinta smiled and stood on her toes and brushed her lips over Ryder's.

'No cheek intended. It's a day for romance, and

14

I hope it might be a celebration for us.'

'Every day's for romance. Or at least it has been since you came to town. I love you, Ryder Francesco.'

'I love you too, now let's dance.'

'You know I'm hopeless. You're the fancy dancer.'

'I wasn't a dancer. I was the stage manager. Come on, I'll teach you.'

'I saw you practising once with Bram. You looked pretty good to me.' Jacinta leaned into Ryder as he placed his hand on the centre of her back. 'Have you heard from Bram yet?' she asked.

'Actually, yes. With all the excitement of the wedding, I forgot to tell you. He called me last night. He assured me he's really well and he did sound upbeat. Clive's visiting him every day.'

'Clive's an absolute gem.'

'He is, and now that I've finally got you to myself, I have something else to tell you later.'

Jacinta leaned back and looked up at Ryder. She still couldn't believe that he'd come back into her life and he hadn't left Augathella since they'd got back together last month.

'What have you got to tell me?'

'Later. Not on the dance floor. Focus on following my feet.'

Jacinta had been so busy helping Sophie with

the last-minute preparations for the wedding over the past two days she hadn't seen much of Ryder.

'Aw, come on, sweetie. You've got me intrigued. Tell me. Come on. Pretty please?'

'What happened to the quiet and shy primary school teacher I fell in love with?'

'I was only quiet because I wasn't happy. Now I'm back to the old Jacinta.' She stood on her toes and brushed her lips across his again. 'Now what do you want to tell me?'

'I love the old Jacinta, but the new one isn't too bad either.' Ryder's grin was wide. Since Bram, his younger brother, had left town and checked into the drug rehab centre in Brisbane, he had been happy.

Jacinta twirled and her bridesmaid dress flared out as Ryder spun her around in a circle. 'Enough teasing. Tell me.'

'Okay. I had a call after I talked to Bram. From Larry.'

'Larry? Do I know a Larry?'

'He was my boss at the Institute in Brisbane. I don't know how you'll feel about what he said, so I said I'd talk to you and get back to him in a day or two.'

'Talk to me?'

'We need to talk about things.'

'Like what?' Jacinta's voice was guarded as the thought of Ryder leaving and going back to

Brisbane came to her mind.

'I'm just going to put those feelers out.'

'Feelers about what?'

Ryder pulled her closer as the volume of the music swelled. 'About my work. There's nothing for me here. I need to go back to my research career.'

'In Brisbane?' Her voice was thick as her body tensed. The thought of Ryder leaving her so soon came as a shock.

'Yes, In Brisbane at the institute. He's offered me a great pay rise, and fabulous conditions.'

'He must value you, and really want you.'

'Yes, he'd like me to come back and work on the project. It's getting pretty close to an exciting finish.'

'And what does your heart tell you, Ryder?'

He looked at her intently. 'My heart tells me that I will do whatever you are happiest doing. If you want to stay out here, we can sort something out, but if you were happy to move to the city with me—'

Jacinta shook her head as she interrupted him. 'We will do whatever we're both happy doing, and if you'd like to go back to the Institute and work on that project I certainly wouldn't mind going back to Brisbane and finding a job in a bigger school.'

'Really?' His voice was husky.

'Really.' She nodded.

'We can always come back for holidays or one day we might even move here, who knows?' Ryder leaned down and took her lips with his. 'I do love you, you know that, don't you?'

'Course I do, as much as I love you. And who knows, we might settle in Brisbane for the long-term and set up home there.'

'As long as we're together, that's all that matters.'

The slow dance music finished and they went to leave the dance floor, but Matt kept the microphone in hand. 'I'm just going to take a fresh air break, folks, and put on some dance music while I'm outside.'

'Let's stay on the dance floor for a while,' Jacinta said.

'Sounds good to me.' Ryan's lips lifted in a grin as he looked over her shoulder. 'I think romance might be in the air tonight. What do you think?' Ryder swung Jacinta around in a circle and she smiled as she saw Ben Riley put his arm around Amelia, and they disappeared into the small alcove behind two of the potted palms.

Jacinta sighed as she caught a glimpse of Ben lowering his head and kissing Amelia soundly.

'I think there might be some news there,' she said. 'You're right. There sure is romance in the air tonight.'

'We'll soon find out.' Ryder grinned as a Blues Brothers song filled the air. 'Ready to shake that tail feather, my love?'

Chapter 4

Fallon and Jon

Fallon jumped to her feet and grabbed Jon's hand. 'Come on, Jon. I love this song.'

Her husband reluctantly put his beer on the table and pulled a face. 'Do I really have to?'

'Yes.' Fallon laughed at the look on his face. 'Come on. Everyone else is up dancing. Look, even Braden is dancing with Callie and you know how much he hates dancing.'

'That's because we're not dancers, sweetheart.' He laughed back with her. 'We're cattlemen. We're used to being on horses and being tough and being out in the paddocks.'

'Yeah, and I know what a softie you really are. Get up here and dance with me, my man.'

Jon stood beside his wife. 'I give in.' They held hands as they walked out to the sound of the Blues Brothers' *Shake your Tail Feather*.

Fallon's fingers and toes tingled with excitement as they approached the dance floor. Many of her friends and family were already out there dancing.

'I love dancing,' she said.

'I know. You've told me.'

She nudged him with her elbow. 'Is that the reason you didn't want to have a real wedding—to get out of the bridal waltz?'

'You're the one who didn't want to have the fussy wedding, Mrs Ingram,' her husband said.

She put a finger on his lips and smiled up at him. 'Ah, yes. I think you're right there.' Fallon laughed again as Jon swooped down and kissed her. He kept her in his arms. 'Right, my dear, show me your moves.'

Fallon linked her arms around Jon's back and her eyes widened as he started dancing. She reached up and spoke loudly over the music. 'You told me you couldn't dance,' she said.

His grin was smug. 'No, I told you, I don't like to dance. My mum made me have lessons when I was in my teens, just for an occasion like this. It's like riding a bike, you never forget how.'

'Well, I'm very pleased that she did.' Fallon looked around her. Braden and Callie were in each other's arms doing a slow waltz to *Shake Your Tail Feather*. She'd never seen that before. Ben and Amelia had their arms around each other, but they were jigging along quite well in time to the music; Sophie and Kent were dancing like champions; they were so good they could win a dance contest.

Contentment filled Fallon as she looked over to one of the tables at the side of the marquee. Mum and Dad were sitting there nursing Ryan, their three-month-old baby. His eyes were wide as he watched the action and listened to the music.

The song changed and *Love Shack* came over the sound system.

'Oh, my favourite!' Fallon said.

'Looks like I'm not going get to get to sit down yet,' Jon said with a mock groan.

'One more and we'll go and sit down.'

'Then I want to talk to you.'

'What about?'

'I found out something from Craig Wilson when we were chatting at the bar before. About some land.'

'You've got me interested. Do you want to go and sit down now?'

'After your favourite.'

At the end of the song, Jon led Fallon past their table to the outside of the marquee.

'We're just going out for a breath of fresh air, Mum. Ryan okay?'

Ruth put her head against Ryan's head and smiled. 'Of course, he's all right. He's with his nanny.'

'Music's not bothering him?'

'He's loving it. He's been jigging around on my lap.'

Fallon laughed. 'He must have his father's dancing genes. Won't be long, Mum.'

They stepped outside the marquee to a brilliant

sunset. The sky was lit up in shades of apricot and deep purple to the west. A low line of clouds gilded the horizon with shards of gold and silver.

The sound of children's laughter came from over near the vegetable garden where Braden's three boys were playing tag with a small group of friends.

Fallon nodded over to the table near where they were playing. Bec Hunter and the singer were sitting close, head to head. 'I've noticed them together a bit in town.'

'He's a nice guy. Moves around a lot apparently, but seems like a decent sort of bloke,' Jon said. 'He asked me at the pub one night if I had any work and I said I'd get back to him. I think he could turn his hand to anything from what he said. He asked Braden too.'

'So what was it you wanted to talk to me about?'

'How would you feel about having our own place, Fallon?'

'Our own place? Property or in town?'

'Property. Craig told me the place on his western boundary is coming on the market.'

'Could we afford it?' she asked as interest sparked. Their own land. How good would that be?

'Possibly. It's pretty rundown and the house is apparently unliveable.'

'Is that Quinn Calthorpe's place? He lives out that way and Sophie was telling me how bad the house is. She doesn't know how he lives in it.'

'No, he's on the northern boundary of Craig's place. I don't know what's going on with Quinn. Since his father died this winter, he's really let the place go.'

'So the house on this one? We could build a new one?' Her eyes were wide as she thought of the possibilities. 'We could make a home. Oh, Jon, I can see it already. I know exactly what sort of house I'd like. You've got me excited. Do you know how much it is?'

Jon shook his head. 'No, but if you think it's a good idea, I'll go and see the Stock and Station agent in Charleville on Monday. That's where it's listed. Apparently, it's very hush-hush for some reason. Craig got wind of it because he saw the owner's son and the agent there yesterday when he was checking a boundary fence. They got into a conversation.'

'So it's only just hitting the market.'

'Yeah, I reckon we should give it a go.'

Fallon stood on her toes and brushed his lips with hers. 'I think that is a fine idea, my dear.'

'I'm very pleased you agree. And yes, we can build our own home there.'

Jon's arms went around her, but he froze as a

piercing scream came from the vegetable garden.

Chapter 5

Amelia and Ben

'Your mother is amazing, Ben,' Amelia said as she came up for air. She ran her fingers through the trailing fronds of the potted palms in front of them. 'I know she organised all the decorating of the marquee.'

'My mother *is* amazing. She can get just about whatever she wants. She's one determined lady when her mind is set on something. Dad knows when to scooter off. When Braden and Callie asked her if they could have the reception in her garden, she was beside herself. The garden is always a picture but she's worked nonstop for the past two months.'

'I know she's been excited, but she does stay focused. I can't get over tropical palm trees in the west of Queensland.' Amelia said, screwing up her nose. 'We're a long way from the tropics.'

'Haven't you ever seen the Charleville palm tree?' Ben asked as his lips nuzzled her neck.

'No. I haven't. What's that?'

'It's one of my favourite landmarks doing the nine-hour drive home from Brisbane. I know I'm getting closer to Augathella when I see that lone palm on the side of the road. I'll show you next time we go to Charleville. Anyway, Mum got these from the guy who's got the date palm property, over on the other side of town. She was over there one day delivering some cakes for the CWA and she spotted a whole lot of new palms growing in pots ready to be put into the paddocks. And of course, she wangled them for the wedding, but he was happy to lend them. Apparently, Braden was a great help to him when he was setting up the property back in the days when Braden was on the council before his wife passed away. He was really pleased to see some innovative stuff being done out here so when the guy asked for help with getting the date palm plantation set up, Braden gave him a hand. So when he heard that Mum wanted the palms for Braden's sister's wedding, he was more than happy to lend whatever he had.'

'It looks fantastic,' Amelia said. 'Especially the way your mum's put all the fairy lights through the marquee. It's magic.' She looked up to the roof of the marquee swathed with netting filled with fairy lights. 'I think it's the most beautiful wedding I've ever been to.'

Ben cleared his throat. 'Um, speaking of weddings, there's um, something I wanted to talk to you about, but I'm not sure if this is the right time.'

'You want to talk to me about something here behind the potted palms?' A frisson of excitement settled in Amelia's chest as she smiled up at Ben.

'Yes, damn it. This is the time. Come over here, sweetheart.' Ben tugged at her hands and led her deeper into the greenery, so they were completely screened from the packed and heaving dance floor. Everybody was up dancing and *Love Shack* was booming over the speakers. Braden and Callie weren't dancing but were standing with their arms around each other, looking into each other's eyes.

Ben grinned. 'Look at that. Ain't love grand?'

'And look at Sophie and Kent.' Amelia said as she peered through the foliage. 'Such a happy couple.'

'And Jacinta and Ryder,' Ben said. He sounded nervous and Amelia turned to look at him. 'I don't know what it is about all these people. Why aren't they dancing? They're all standing there looking gooey-eyed at each other.'

Amelia giggled as he pulled at her hand. 'Gooey-eyed?'

'Yes. Now come over here. I want to look all gooey-eyed at you,' Ben said.

'Why do you want to look at me? We need to get out there and dance.'

'First things first.' Ben cleared his throat again and Amelia frowned.

'What's up, Ben? Don't you like dancing? Is that what you want to talk about? Or do you want to ask Matt if you can sing too? I'm sure everyone would be happy if you got up there at some stage during the night.'

'Amelia, stop prattling.'

Her eyes widened as Ben shook his head and dropped to one knee behind the largest potted palm He reached into his pocket and pulled out a small blue velvet box.

'I put this in here because I just had a feeling that tonight was the right night, like I said, love is in the air. Amelia, my darling girl. Will you—' Ben held her hands tightly and looked up at her and her love for this man raced through her. It was a physical feeling in her chest. Her heart picked up a beat and she swallowed, hoping, knowing, praying what he was about to ask her. 'I will,' she said before he could finish. 'Oh Ben, yes I will.'

'You will you do me the honour of being my wife?' Ben's eye's let up; he was always happy, but this was the happiest she'd ever seen him.

'Of course, I will. I thought you were never going to ask,' she said before Ben could get up. Amelia dropped to her knees in front of him and put her arms around his neck as his lips took hers in a long kiss.

'Can I stop kissing you to put the ring on your finger?'

'You can.'

Ben flipped the box open and the myriad of fairy lights above them sent shards of light onto the large gem.

'Oh, Ben,' Amelia breathed.

He slid the ring onto her finger, and she looked down inside.

'It's perfect.' The blue sapphire, surrounded by little diamonds, sparkled up at her and she looked up at him and kissed him again.

'You're perfect, Amelia, and I'm looking forward to spending the rest of my life with you.'

Chapter 6

Reg

The music was playing some loud rubbish about a love shack and old Reg shook his head. What on earth was a love shack, and did they really need that rubbish music at a wedding? What happened to good old Elvis love songs? There was no decent music these days. In fact, he hadn't heard a truly decent song since Chad Morgan had come to town about forty years ago and sung the *Duckinwilla Dance*.

Now that's a song they could dance to. He'd go up and ask that young fella singing if he knew it when he came back inside. He'd even ask one of the lasses for a dance if he'd sing that one. Then again, maybe Ben Riley would know it. But it looked like he was otherwise occupied.

Old Reg had been overwhelmed when he'd been invited to the wedding, and he didn't care that he was tired and it was way past his usual bedtime; he'd be able to talk about this night for weeks. His eyes didn't miss a trick as he watched the proceedings from his chair in prime position close to the bridal table.

Romance was in the air.

He'd been right about the girl of Mason, and that dancer fella. He'd heard they were engaged

31

already. Seemed quick, but the gossip was they'd known each other before.

He grinned and nodded as he watched Doc Higgins guide the midwife into a dark corner and swoop her into a long kiss. Nurse Adnum was flushed when they reappeared. She waved to Reg when she saw him watching; everyone else was too busy jiving about on the dance floor to see what was going on under their very noses. Like most of the stuff that happened in town. If you watched, you saw it all. Reg liked the midwife; Laura always stopped to talk to him in the street when she walked to the hospital.

Reg smiled when he saw Ben Riley kneel down in front of that pretty Amelia who'd spent time chatting to Reg at the billy cart races last Easter. From where he was sitting he could see between the fronds and he nodded as Ben pulled a little box out of his pocket. Looked like there was another wedding coming up in Augathella.

Braden and Callie Cartwright had their arms around each other, talking together over the loud music. Reg looked around. There was no sign of their boys. As long as they weren't in Jenny Riley's garden, he thought. She'd just about spank them if they damaged any plants. That woman had a green thumb. In fact, she had ten green fingers. No one would ever think they were in the outback.

Reg sat up straight and watched as the other nurse from the hospital hurried into the tent.

No, not a tent, he told himself. It had some fancy name. A marquee, that's what it was. A bit flash for a little town like theirs.

As soon as the singer fellow had gone out for a breath of fresh air, Nurse Hunter had followed him like a shot. Reg suspected there might be something going on there too. Since that Matt had turned up in town and started working behind the bar in the pub, Nurse Hunter had spent a fair few nights in there chatting to him. They must have had a blue, Reg thought, but he narrowed his eyes as she hurried over to Doc Higgins and grabbed his arm and spoke urgently to him. No one else noticed Harry Higgins rush outside looking mighty worried.

Reg's curiosity got the better of him, and he stood and shuffled out of the tent. He needed to know everything that happened at the wedding so he could tell his stories at the pub next week.

Jon and Fallon Ingram and the Cartwright kids were beside the vegetable garden where the kids had been playing when Reg had gone outside for a durrie a while back. The two bigger boys were standing over their little brother who was lying on the ground. Surely he hadn't gone to sleep on the ground. Jon Ingram was crouched beside him and as Reg watched, Fallon put her arms around the two big boys.

Strange that.

That singer fellow lay on the ground too. The doc and Nurse Hunter were kneeling beside him.

Reg's eyes widened as he saw the spreading pool of blood under the fella's head.

The last thing Augathella needed was a death at a wedding, Reg thought as he headed inside to tell Braden something was very wrong.

Chapter 7
Harry

'Please step back a little, Braden, and let me check Peter.'

Dr Harry Higgins focused on keeping his voice calm and controlled as he kneeled beside the still body of the little boy on the ground. When Braden had come running out of the marquee, he'd taken his son from Nigel and Rory, and laid him in the recovery position.

'He's breathing, Harry. I checked. I was ready to start resuscitation, but there's no need. Petie wake up. Open your eyes, bub.'

Harry glanced back at Braden, as he moved away just enough to let him kneel beside Petie. Braden's face was chalk-white and his lips were tight as he fought for control.

The two older boys, Rory and Nigel, stood behind their father, tears rolling down their faces as Harry leaned over Petie, quickly checking his breathing and pulse.

Braden straightened. 'Rory, can you please take Nigel inside and find Aunty Sophie and tell her that I want her to look after both of you? Inside. Ask her, tell her—' his voice broke— 'tell her to send Callie out. Please.'

Nigel's sobs filled the air as the two boys did as

they were told. Braden crouched back down beside Harry. His hands were covered with blood.

'Braden? Do you have a clean handkerchief?'

Braden dug into his trouser pockets, where there was a brand new handkerchief, courtesy of Callie.

He managed to hold it together at the sight of the white handkerchief that she had ironed for him, especially for the wedding. Callie had bought and prepared new outfits for all of them. She had her pale pink matron of honour dress, which Sophie had insisted on buying, but she'd gone online shopping a few weeks ago and bought outfits for Braden and the three boys. His eyes stung as he handed the clean, pressed handkerchief over.

'Yes, I have,' he said roughly.

'Okay, I want you to slip it under the back of Peter's head. I'm just going to move him very gently. I want you to press it against the wound to stop the bleeding. The laceration is at the base of his hair just above the top of his neck. Okay? Are you able to do that for me, Braden?'

'I'm fine, Doc. I'm okay. We just need to get him to wake up.' Despite his assurance that he was calm, Braden's voice hitched. 'Harry, please don't let me lose my little boy.'

Harry nodded and gently lifted Petie's head about five centimetres. Braden managed to slip the folded handkerchief where the doctor had directed.

Harry tried not to react as he saw how quickly the blood soaked the fabric. Petie was breathing evenly, but he was still unconscious.

'Do we know what happened?'

Braden's voice was tight. 'The boys said the gust of wind lifted a sheet of iron off that small gardening shed over there. It hit Matt's shoulder as he tried to get Petie out of the way, but clipped the back of Petie's head and then he fell backwards onto the concrete edge of the garden.'

Harry focused on keeping the worry from his expression. He'd suspected it was more than a laceration. An impact injury was not good. 'Braden, I'll look after him here. Can you please go in and get Laura for me and as soon as you tell her, call the ambulance.' He glanced over at Matt lying on the ground. The young man was conscious, but Harry could see the pool of blood, beneath his right shoulder. Bec Hunter had ripped the long skirt of her dress and had a pad pressed against the open wound. It was going to need a lot of stitches, and most probably surgery. That type of surgery was beyond Harry with the minimal staff he had at the local hospital, and he was going to have to get Matt to Charleville. He would possibly need an orthopaedic surgeon.

'Tell them to call Charleville and get the Royal Flying Doctor Service in the air.'

Harry was barely aware of Braden leaving, as he gently examined little Peter Cartwright.

His breathing was even, but his face was white, and there was a jagged gash on the back of his head, from his neck into his hairline. As Harry probed lightly, he tensed as his fingers encountered a soft depression in the base of his skull. Petie's white shirt was soaked with blood. He was deeply unconscious and when Harry had gently lifted his eyelids once he was satisfied his pulse and breathing were regular, Petie's pupils had responded differently, and there was a trickle of fluid coming out of his left ear.

'Bec, can you please move over here and monitor Petie while I have a quick look at Matt.'

Bec's face was ashen as she came and sat beside the little boy.

'He's not good, is he?' she said quietly.

'No, it's quite a serious head injury. I suspect a fractured skull.' As he spoke another strong gust of wind blew across the paddocks, red dust swirling in the air. The marquee tilted and there was yelling from inside. 'If this wind keeps up, we're going to have some more injuries if that marquee shifts more. I hate to say it, but I think it needs to be cleared.'

'Doctor Higgins, if this wind keeps up the Flying Doctor isn't going to get in the air,' Bec said.

'I know.'

Harry moved across to Matt. 'Are you with us, Matt?'

'I'm okay, Doc. Don't worry about me. Look after the little fella.' Matt's voice was thready, and Harry could see his pain. As he quickly examined him, it became clear that he'd lost a lot of blood already. He needed urgent attention.

They both did.

Harry hadn't felt this helpless since . . . since he'd sat by the lake in Newcastle knowing there was nothing he could do to save his beautiful wife.

Chapter 8

Half an hour later

Bec stepped back and put her hand up to stop her hair from flying across her face. The wop-wop of the helicopter filled the air and the updraft caused by its ascent added to the already intense wind.

The ambulance with Matt had just left for the local hospital; for once, they'd been lucky. Both patients were on the way to specialist help. Now they had to deal with the fallout that was left behind.

The Royal Flying Doctor helicopter had been in the air on the way back to Charleville after dropping a patient back to Blackall, and it had been almost to Augathella when the call went out for medical help for Petie Cartwright. The chopper had been able to land and the paramedics had assisted immediately.

The proximity of the helicopter had probably saved the little boy's life. When Bec had met Doc Higgins' eyes above the still figure on the grass she'd known the prognosis was very bad.

'We can't go. We're not going.' Sophie's shrill voice had Bec swinging around as the helicopter receded into the distance leaving only the roar of the increasing wind.

'You can and you are.' Callie moved into Bec's line of sight. Her shoulders were stooped and her face was streaked with tears. Kent and Sophie had held her close as the helicopter took off with Braden and Petie on board.

Rory and Nigel were in Kimberley Riordan's care; she lived close to the Riley's place. Kim had suggested it would be best to get them away from the scene where they could see the blood and the medical equipment as the helicopter approached. Fallon and Jon had gone with Kim.

'No, Sophie, don't be ridiculous.'

'Listen to me carefully, Callie. I'll say it once more, we are *not* leaving you.'

'You can't put your honeymoon off. You've booked your flights to Fiji and your accommodation, and you've paid for everything.'

'And do you think we would enjoy one minute of that when Petie is in a critical condition? Sweetie, you're not thinking straight.'

Bec's heart went out to Sophie. Tears rolled down her face and bloodstains marred her beautiful wedding dress from where she'd leaned over to kiss the little boy's cheek before he was loaded onto the helicopter.

'I was mother to that little boy for two years, and there's no way I will go away and leave him. Or Braden and Rory and Nigel. Or you, Callie.'

Bec could see the expression on Callie's face as she let out an anguished cry. She knew that Callie loved those three boys as though they were her own. When she'd married Braden a few months ago, she'd not only become a wife but also the stepmother to the three energetic little boys. Even though she'd had less time caring for Petie than Sophie had when Braden had handed the three boys over to his younger sister after his first wife's death, Bec knew that Callie adored him. She adored the three of them, and she was a wonderful mother.

Callie crumpled and Kent grabbed for her before she could fall to the ground.

'Bec, can you help us?' Sophie called.

'Of course.' Bec ran across and supported Callie on her other side. 'Come on Callie, sit on the ground for a while and we'll get you into a car; somewhere where you can lie down for a while. Do you feel faint or sick?'

Sophie gestured to Bec over Callie's bowed hand. She tapped her own stomach and mouthed silently, 'She's pregnant.'

Callie gripped Bec's hands and shook her head. 'No. Yes, just a little bit faint. I saw stars for a minute but I'm okay now. I have to look after the boys and I have to drive to Charleville. Braden will need me. But first, I'll have to go out to Kilcoy Station because he'll need a change of clothes, and he'll need—'

'Sweetie. Stop, take a deep breath and stop

planning. We need to wait.' Bec kept her voice low and calm. 'You need to take some time to calm down. I know how hard it is for you'—she looked at Sophie and Kent—'for all of you, but it's going to be a while before we know anything. There's a chance they'll take Petie to the Children's Hospital in Brisbane once they've done some scans in Charleville.'

'No, I want to go to Charleville. I want to be with them.'

'He'll be all right, Callie, he will. He's a strong little bugger,' Sophie said determinedly.

'How about you all come to my place? We can pick up Nigel and Rory from Kim's on the way,' Bec said. 'It keeps you in town rather than out on your stations, and then when any news comes through, you can decide who's going where. The most important thing is to stay positive and calm. Petie's in good hands. There's nothing more we can do here, except look after those two little boys, and you, Callie. And you too, Sophie. '

Bec's emotions were in turmoil. She knew she was needed here, but she wanted to get to the hospital as quickly as she could.

Matt had lost consciousness while they were waiting for the paramedics to arrive, but he came around quickly. She wanted to be with him, and that confused her. It wasn't because he needed medical help; she just wanted to be with *him*.

'He's lost a lot of blood,' Doctor Higgins said. 'I'm wondering whether we give him some blood here before we take him down to Charleville. I'll call and see if he can go down tonight. We'll decide our action then.'

When the ambulance arrived, there was a quick consultation with Dr Higgins, and the decision was made to take him to the local hospital here at Augathella for a quick blood transfusion, depending on his blood type.

'Hopefully, we'll have some blood,' Dr Higgins said. 'Matt? Do you know what your blood type is?'

Matt's reply was faint and Bec wondered why a strange expression crossed his face before he spoke. 'I don't know. I knew once, but I can't remember now,' he said vaguely.

'No matter. We'll get you into ED,' the doctor said. Within minutes, Matt was in the ambulance and the doctor had gestured to Laura to bring his car around.

'Can you meet us in emergency, please, Nurse Hunter?'

'I will. I'll just check on Callie and follow you.'

Bec was still coming to terms with the feelings she had for Matt, but she didn't have time to dwell on that now. 'Kent, is your vehicle here?'

'Yes, it's around the back of the shed.'

'You take Callie and Sophie, and pick the boys up, and I'll meet you there later. The back door's unlocked. Just make yourselves at home. Tea and coffee are in the cupboard above the kettle, and there's a bottle of brandy on the shelf in the dining room if you need it. Clean towels are in the linen cupboard outside the bathroom for the boys to have a shower.'

'There's a change of clothes for them in our car,' Callie said dully.

'I'll go to the hospital and see if Dr Higgins needs me first.' Bec ran shaking hands down the front of her beautiful dress. She'd bought it in Brisbane especially to wear to Sophie's wedding. The pale green silk was now stained with blood from both Petie and Matt, with a ragged hem where she'd torn it to make the pad against Matt's wound. The dress was destined for the garbage bin now, but that meant nothing in the scheme of things.

Matt would be all right, but his shoulder injury was a worry; it could have implications for the use of his arm. He was travelling around Australia in a beat-up old van, picking up seasonal work where he could. Bec couldn't understand the attraction Matt held for her; when she wasn't with him, she could talk sense to herself. He was not the sort of man she'd ever be interested in. When she was with him, she felt . . . it was hard to define even for herself.

She felt something she'd never felt before. Satisfied. Complete. Totally happy when he was there.

But she couldn't understand why.

Matt Randall was a drifter. He had no proper job, no training, and no permanent home, and he was very reticent about anything personal.

'Live in the moment, Bec. It's all that matters,' he'd said more than once.

She also assumed he had very little money behind him by the state of his van parked at the side of the pub. Again that was none of her business. He was just a man whom she'd met, and become friends with and Matt would soon move on, and her emotions would get back to normal.

'All a man needs is fresh air and his guitar,' he'd told her holding her gaze with his deep blue eyes, the afternoon they'd gone to the river for a picnic. She fought hard to stop her emotions from being involved but no matter how much logic told her he wasn't good for her, whenever she was with him, common sense went out the window. She couldn't understand how someone could be so aimless, yet so happy and content in his simple life. She'd go stir-crazy living like that.

'Well, a girl needs more than that,' she'd told him that first night she'd met him at the Tambo pub when Jacinta had dragged her up there because

Ryder's dance troupe was performing.

She could still see Matt propping his chin in his hand only centimetres away from her face, as he held her eyes across the bar. She could feel his warm breath on her cheek when he spoke. 'So tell me what a girl like you *does* need, lovely lady.'

They'd had the bar to themselves; once the music had started everyone had gone out the back where the male revue was performing. It wasn't fair. Matt had the looks, the voice, and the physique that made him an almost perfect male specimen. He looked more like a movie star than a guy wandering around the outback. If only he had ambition.

A warm rush of feeling had filled her, and her heartbeat had raced as he'd held his eyes. In that moment, she'd known that their relationship would probably go past friendship if he stayed around. She wouldn't be able to resist him, and that confused her.

Bec had never felt that sort of physical attraction to anyone so strongly. She wasn't a novice in the sexual department. The fleeting relationships and the occasional one-night stand with male friends when she'd been at uni in Brisbane had been fun, but since she'd moved home to Augathella, her focus had been her work and study.

Pushing the memory of that night away, Bec turned to give Callie, Kent, and Sophie some privacy as they stood in a tight huddle talking about their best option. The evening was filled with the noise of cars driving down the drive as guests headed home in shock.

As she turned, Bec's eyes widened at the macabre scene in front of her. There were still a few people standing outside the marquee which had been evacuated before the helicopter arrived. That meant that there had been a whole audience as the two patients were respectively loaded into the helicopter and an ambulance. Faces were stricken and many of the women cried. The men pitched in and helped secure the marquee on the side where it had shifted. Some of those who'd helped lift Petie and Matt onto the stretchers had bloodstains on their clothes. Several men had lifted and moved the rogue sheet of roofing that had caused the injuries. It was now safely in the paddock adjacent to the shed, held down with bricks on top.

A few groups stood outside the wedding marquee which still sat at an awkward angle from where one side had blown out.

Old Reg from the pub was sitting on a plastic chair outside the doorway, much the same as he did every day outside the pub, but the elderly man's face was white and his eyes wide.

Bec hurried over to him. 'Are you okay, Reg? You look a bit pale on it, mate.'

Reg nodded. 'The old ticker's racing a bit, but I'm okay, thanks, love. It just threw me a bit to see that poor little fella so badly hurt. He's not good, is it, Bec? Is he going to die?'

'The paramedics will look after him and the doctors in Charleville will take care of him.' Bec hoped that was the case but she was worried about upsetting Reg more. 'We don't know yet, Reg. We won't know until we hear more. It could be a while.'

'Those poor buggers.' Reg shook his head. 'With all Braden's been through, and on Sophie's wedding day. On this one day that should've been happy. A bloody freak accident and look what's happened.'

'I know. It's sad,' Bec said. 'But look on the positive side.'

'Is there one?' Reg squinted up at her and she was pleased to see a bit more colour in his face.

'They're both alive, and they're in good hands, and there will be some happy memories of the wedding and reception after this is all over.'

'How's your fella?'

'My fella?' Bec frowned. 'Do you mean Matt? The singer?'

'Yeah, I meant the singer. I thought he was your fella. You've been spending a lot of time with him this past month. You can't put anything past old

Reg, love. I don't miss a trick.'

'Well, you've read that trick wrong.' Bec's voice was quite firm. 'Matt is a friend, but not my fella. He's got a big cut on his shoulder, and I think there might have been some muscle damage. I'd say that he'll end up in surgery at Charleville if they can get a specialist to fly in.'

'Good.'

'Okay, Reg. I'm heading across to the hospital now. Would you like a lift back into town?'

'That would be good. I'd appreciate that. But listen, before we go, maybe you need to see to Jenny Riley.'

'Jenny Riley? What's wrong? Is she hurt too?'.

'No, she's not hurt, but she's pretty distraught about what's happened.'

Bec nodded. 'Of course, she would be. But it was an accident. It was the wind and no one could have predicted what was going to happen.'

'I'll just sit here for a minute. You go over and see if you can help her. I think she might need sedating or something.' A ghost of a grin lifted his mouth. 'Or a good double brandy.'

Bec went looking for Jenny. The entrance to the marquee, where trails of fairy lights had been strung out over the door, had ripped up one side. The lights had been trampled into the ground as the guests had fled from the toppling marquee. White linen napkins swirled in the red dust as the wind gusted again.

Ben and Amelia were sitting with Jenny on the back steps of the homestead, with Tom, Jenny's husband, standing in front of them with his hand on her shoulder.

Relief crossed Ben's face as he looked up. 'Bec, have they gone to the hospital?'

Bec nodded without going into details. 'Yes.' She stood in front of the steps. 'Jenny, it's okay. Just take a deep breath. Are you feeling faint or anything?'

'Jen's had a few heart issues over the years,' Tom said. 'I'm worried that this stress is going to kick an attack off.'

'Heart issues,' Ben interrupted. 'Why didn't I know that?'

'Hush, Ben. Not the time,' Bec said quietly. 'What sort of heart issues have you had, Jenny?'

Jenny lifted one hand and gave a dismissive wave. 'I'm okay. I'm on medication for SVT and it's working.'

'What's SVT?' Ben demanded.

'Just sometimes my heart beats really fast when I get stressed and then I get really tired. I'm okay. I'm just worried about poor little Petie and Matt.'

'You know none of this is your fault, don't you?' Bec said. 'It was an unforeseen accident.'

As Jenny nodded, Bec reached for her wrist and put her fingers on her pulse point. Jenny seemed unaware of her touch as she stared past Bec's shoulder.

'I do know that it was just a bloody horrible accident. I didn't even know that the roof was loose on that little shed. The wind's been blowing on that shed for years and years and the roof never once lifted. Why the hell did it have to happen today? Why did the boys have to be out there? Why did it have to do this on Sophie's day?' Tears filled her eyes. 'And I do worry about the marquee though. I hope the firm put it up to standard. We could get sued.'

'Worrying's not going to help anyone,' Bec said as she let go of Jenny's arm. 'Go inside. Almost everyone's gone now. We'll get all this sorted when the wind drops. Tom? Keep a close eye on Jenny. Make her lie down, and if there's any sign of any tachycardia or faintness, call the ambulance. Actually, on second thought, bring her straight to the hospital because the ambos could be on their way to Charleville with Matt.'

'I'm okay,' Jenny insisted. 'I know when I'm getting an attack and I don't feel like it now. I'm just bloody upset.'

'Okay, well, take care. I'm off to the hospital now. I'll let you know as soon as there is any news.

I'm dropping Reg off at his place on the way.'

Chapter 9

Kent and Sophie soon had Callie in the car and were heading to Bec's house. Bec stood next to the driver's window when Kent called her over.

'Let us know if there's any news,' he said.

'If I hear anything I'll call my home phone or do you want to give me your mobile?'

'Either. I'll give you my mobile now and I'll give you Callie's too, just in case you can't get onto mine as soon as you hear anything.'

'You okay, Kent?'

'Yeah, Bec. I'm fine. As good as can be expected. I have to be. I'll look after the girls, and Rory and Nigel. Callie is itching to get down to Charleville, but I've talked her into coming back and having a cup of tea first and just sitting for a while until we find out what's happening.'

'That's a wise plan,' Bec said. 'I imagine that we'll know pretty soon.' She reached up to the driver's window and squeezed his arm. 'Take care of yourself too, mate.'

'Thanks, Bec. Hopefully, talk to you very soon.'

Bec collected Reg and they headed for her car which was parked out on the road. Most of the cars had gone now, and she groaned when she saw a tree branch across the bonnet. The wind this afternoon had been incredible. It hadn't been forecast, and Bec had never seen anything gusting this much in all the years she lived in the west. Red dust whirled along the road in an ongoing procession of willie-willies as they approached her car.

'I'll help you lift that off, love,' he said.

'No. You get in the car.' She clicked the remote to unlock it. 'I don't want any more injuries today.'

Surprisingly he did as he was told. Bec suspected Reg was a lot more shaken than he was letting on. Luckily the branch was not too heavy and she was able to lift it off easily. Thankfully there were no dents. Just a few scratches in the Duco that should polish out but it didn't matter.

Bec jumped in and drove down Roselyn Road, past the racecourse until the road split and then turned right into Cavanagh Street. Reg's house was at the end of the road, and she waited while he climbed out.

'You take care of yourself, Reg.'

'You too, love. Call in and let me know when there's any news, won't you?'

Bec nodded. 'I will. I just hope it's all good news.'

Reg would be like the town crier, and he'd be in his usual chair outside the pub to let everyone know how things were progressing.

Waiting until he unlocked his front door and disappeared inside, she drove the short distance to the hospital and pulled up in the staff car park.

As she parked, Bec noticed there was no ambulance in the emergency bay, and she wondered what had happened. Surely they wouldn't have taken Matt to Charleville already.

She hurried out of the car and went around to the back of the hatchback and pulled out the pair of joggers she always kept in there. Stepping out of her sparkly shoes she pulled the joggers on and grimaced as she looked at her ripped bloodstained dress and then down to her white running shoes.

Appearance didn't matter. It was all about being comfortable. She hurried into the building through the staff entrance at the side, keen to see Matt, and find out how he was. Heading straight to the sink, she had a good wash, removing the blood and dust from her hands and arms before she headed down to the emergency department.

To her relief, the curtains were open and she spotted Matt in the third cubicle from the end. Harry was standing beside him.

Harry was talking quietly to him and Bec waited at the edge of the curtain until he'd finished speaking.

Harry turned around to leave. 'Nurse Hunter. Good to see you here.'

'I was surprised to see the ambulance gone,' she said. 'I thought Matt must have gone already.'

Harry pulled a face. 'Yes, there has been a car accident on the other side of town. A minor accident according to the call in, but they're bringing in the driver.' He nodded to Matt. 'This young man was able to find his blood type in his wallet so we're getting a transfusion ready to put up. Luckily he's O positive and we have it on hand. He'll be ready for surgery as soon as he gets there if we get his blood volume and red cell mass optimised before he goes. There's a good chance of surgery tonight. We're in luck. The locum orthopaedic surgeon is in town and she's due to fly out tomorrow. I'm waiting for her to call back.'

Before Bec could answer, Harry's mobile rang in his pocket; he pulled it out and nodded as he walked away.

Bec walked across to the side of the bed. Matt's eyes were closed, and there was a cannula in his arm.

She sat in the plastic chair next to the side of the bed and observed him. His eyes were closed, and his long lashes fanned his cheeks. Dark shadows marred his usually clear skin and his mouth was set in a tight line as he endured the pain. She wondered if painkillers were going into the infusion yet.

'Marianne. Marianne.' Matt jerked as he called

out and tried to lift the arm the cannula was in.

Bec frowned and put her hand on his good arm. 'It's okay, Matt. Everything is fine. You're in the hospital.'

His eyes opened wide and he stared at her. 'What are you doing here?' His words were slurred.

'I work here. I think you were dreaming.'

He closed his eyes again and took a breath, and she waited.

'Yeah, I was.' His usual bright voice was flat.

'Are you in much pain?'

'Not since the doc put the good gear in the drip.'

'As long as it's helping.'

'Maybe I can take some home.' Matt's attempt at a joke was feeble.

Before Bec could answer Harry appeared at the end of the bed.

'Good news, Matt we've got a surgeon already down at Charleville. Dr Ruth Haas has been over here on her fortnightly visit and you're in luck. She's not flying to Brisbane till tomorrow so once the transfusion's done, we'll put you in the ambulance and take you down to Charleville.'

'How's the little boy?' Matt asked. 'Any news yet?'

'No, no news there, yet,' Harry answered, 'but it's good to hear there's a couple of specialists on hand down there at the hospital for the weekend.

He's in good hands. Can I have a word, Nurse Hunter?'

Bec stood and squeezed Matt's good hand. It was killing her seeing him in such pain. 'I'll see you soon, Matt.'

His eyes were closed and he nodded.

Bec followed Harry out to the corridor.

'What's wrong, Harry? I'm sorry, I mean, what's wrong, Dr Higgins? I'm still in wedding mode.'

'It's okay, Bec, you know it's Harry to you. I was hoping you would go down to Charleville. The paramedics can look after him there but I was wondering if I could ask you to go down in your car and keep an eye on him. I'm a bit worried about the state he's in. He was really agitated when we brought him in. It would be good to have someone he knows with him after the surgery. Especially if the news isn't good.'

'Agitated?' Bec asked. 'That's out of character. He's always so chilled.'

'He's been saying some strange things. I know you two have become friends since he's come to town, haven't you?'

Bec nodded. 'Yes, we've become mates very quickly.' She frowned. 'I'm due on the morning shift here tomorrow.'

'That's okay. I've already checked the roster

and spoken to Laura. She's happy to fill in.'

'It will keep everyone's mind off Petie, being at work. Being focused,' Bec said.

'Jesus, what a balls-up of an afternoon,' Harry said running a hand through his short-cropped grey hair.

'You okay, doc?'

'I'm okay,' he said with a sigh, 'but I'm bloody worried about that little boy. The signs weren't good at all. I just hope they made it to Charleville.'

Bec closed her eyes and held her breath. She'd known it was bad, but to hear Harry voice it, she knew how serious Petie's condition was.

'We can just hope and pray for the best, that's all we can do.'

Harry nodded and they stood quietly for a moment, each lost in their thoughts.

'Go home and get yourself some gear packed, and changing your clothes may be a good idea.' Harry gestured to the front of her bloodstained dress. 'If they do operate on him tonight, please don't drive home in the dark. No matter what happens. The hospital can pay your fuel and accommodation bill. I'd send you in the ambulance, but you wouldn't be able to get back.'

'No worries. I've got a house down there.'

Harry raised his eyebrows. 'That's handy.'

'Yeah, it was my grandma's house for a long

time. I should sell it but I've never got around to going down and cleaning it out. Too many memories.'

'Good ones, I hope,' His smile was gentle and for the umpteenth time Bec thought how lucky Augathella had been the day Dr Harry came to town. There had been times before his arrival when there hadn't been a doctor on duty.

'Yes. good ones.'

'If you'd rather stay in a motel, do that.'

'No, it's about time I faced the house,' Bec said. 'It will make me get myself organised.'

'It's hard to clean out a house and personal possessions when women has gone.'

Bec knew that Harry's wife had passed away a few years ago, but he never spoke of it. She was really pleased that he and Laura had got together. Harry had a spring in his step these days.

'Okay, Bec. You drive carefully and give me a call when you get down there. Keep me in the loop with Matt.'

'And you keep me in the loop with Petie.' Bec couldn't help herself. She stood up on her toes and kissed Harry's cheek.

'Thanks, Dr Harry, we were very lucky that you were there this afternoon.'

Harry's cheeks flushed red, and he shook his head.

'We need more than luck in this, Bec. We need some divine intervention.'

Chapter 10

Sophie

Sophie leaned down and rested her face against Nigel's flushed cheek. He was a little bit warm and she frowned as she lifted her head and placed her hand on his forehead. One of the other boys getting sick was the last thing they needed. After a moment, she realised he was simply warm from being snug under the blankets. She was worrying unnecessarily.

Rory and Nigel were in the spare room at Bec's house, where the two twin beds had been made up. Nigel had gone to sleep in the car and when Sophie had found the made-up beds, Kent had carried Nigel to bed. He hadn't stirred. Bec had called in briefly, had a quick shower, packed a bag and left, telling them she was going to Charleville Hospital to be with Matt. Sophie hadn't been surprised. She'd seen how close they were when she'd done those couple of shifts at the pub bistro for Sean last week.

Rory yawned as he lay on top of the covers on the chenille cover of the other bed. Sophie stepped across and sat beside him, her fingers lightly stroking his hair.

'You okay, buddy?'

'Sort of, Aunty Sophie. I can't stop worrying about Petie. He screamed so loud when that roof hit

63

him. He yelled out really loud when he tried to run away when it was coming down on him, but it was moving too fast to get out of the way. That man pushed him because, you know what, all I can think of if . . . if . . . if he hadn't pushed Petie down, I reckon it could've—what's that word, that big word, that awful thing?'

'I don't know, darling. What big word?' Sophie frowned wondering what was in Rory's head.

'When your head gets cut off. I saw on one of those horrible cartoons with a thing called a guillotine. Callie won't let us watch it anymore.'

'I'm glad to hear that and don't worry about that word. We don't need to think about it. It didn't happen to Petie. Are you sleepy? Have you had enough to eat?'

'My tummy is rolling and I felt sick for a little. I thought I was going to throw up, but I am sleepy now. Aunty Sophie?

'Yes, sweetie?'

'I know I'm the oldest, and I am big now, but will you sit with me here until I go to sleep?'

'Course I will, sweetheart.'

Rory snuggled into the pillow and closed his eyes, and Sophie smoothed her hand over his hair as his breathing evened out.

She looked across at Nigel and then back at Rory. Two of her three beautiful nephews. Little boys that had seen way too much sadness in their young lives. Dear God, please don't let any more grief impact them.

She loved these boys with all her heart, and the thought of Petie away from them in a strange hospital, and critically ill, broke her heart.

Suddenly Rory jerked.

'What is it, mate?'

'I was just going to sleep, and I started to have a little dream, about Mummy. Not Callie-Mummy but about Mummy, our real mummy. And then I thought of something.'

Sophie's throat clogged as she held back tears. 'Yes, sweetie, what was it?'

'If Petie dies, he'll go and be with our real mummy, won't he? She'll look after him, but oh, Aunty Sophie, I'd miss him so much. He can be a little tease, and even though he's my brother, I do love him. But I never told him that.'

Sophie couldn't hold back the tears anymore, and they rolled down her cheek as she lifted Rory and put her arms around him, pulling him close. That little boy smell of damp hair and soap surrounded her.

'We're not going to worry about that. We are going to think happy thoughts and we're gonna send every positive one we can. Can you do that?'

Rory nodded.

'Petie is on his way to a place to help him get better. He's at the hospital now in Charleville with Daddy and they'll be looking after him really well. I'm just waiting for a phone call from Daddy and we'll know what's happening.'

'Will you wake me up and tell me if anything happens?' Rory asked, his eyes wide and his lips trembling.

'I promise.'

Sophie laid him back down and tucked the light blanket around him. 'Now try to go back to sleep and think happy thoughts. Okay?'

'Okay.' Rory's voice was sleepy again.

No child should have to go through this, Sophie cursed to herself. Rory had been too young when Julia had been killed in the horse accident to bear the amount of grief that he was now old enough to carry. He was old enough to understand that Petie had been badly hurt and that there was a chance he wouldn't pull through.

Sophie shook herself mentally; she wasn't going to think that way, but she'd just told Rory they needed to be positive on every count and she had to follow her own advice.

'I love you, Aunty Sophie.' His eyes fluttered closed. 'You looked really pretty today and I didn't tell you.'

'Thank you, sweetheart, now hush and go to

sleep.'

Rory was soon asleep, and Sophie tucked the blanket around him again. He'd already pulled his arms out.

Leaving the door open she made her way out to the living room. Nobody was in there, and she walked through to the kitchen. Kent and Callie were sitting at the table, a pot of tea covered with a knotted tea cosy in the shape of a red rooster. It was the last thing she would have expected Bec to have; she was very much contemporary in her taste. The house was decorated in a minimal style, and the bright tea cosy contrasted with the muted tones of the kitchen.

Sophie opened a couple of cupboards before she found a mug, sat down and poured herself a cup of tea.

Callie was cradling her cup between her fingers. Her face was white, and it was amazing that already she appeared gaunt, her cheeks pinched.

How long ago had she looked rosy and happy? Sophie glanced at the watch. It had just gone seven and at noon, seven hours ago, Callie had refused a glass of champagne. Her eyes had sparkled and a secretive smile danced on her lips.

Sophie had guessed she was pregnant, and now it was hard to accept that happy glowing face had turned into this strained expression in a matter of hours.

Three mobile phones sat on the table, waiting for a call, but the silence was deafening.

Chapter 11

It was seven-thirty by the time Matt's blood transfusion was complete. The ambulance had come back to the hospital, dropping off a patient with minor injuries.

Dr Harry examined the patient and passed her into the care of Laura.

'You need to go home and get some sleep. How are you, Harry?'

'How do I look?' he said. 'As bad as I feel?'

'You look exhausted.' Laura said.

'I'm okay. A cup of coffee will keep me going, and I'll wait till Matt heads off to Charleville before I unscrew the top of the new whiskey bottle.'

'Bec's just getting him ready for the transfer now. The ambos are having something to eat. We've had a big day, and there's no relief staff.'

He rolled his eyes. 'I don't know what's happening to our health system. Why we can't get staff? No doctors, no nurses. It's bad enough running a small hospital. I can't imagine what it'd be like in the city these days with hundreds of patients and COVID still casting its shadow over everything. The pressure is horrendous.'

'Come into the staffroom and I'll make you that

coffee,' Laura said looping her arm through his.

Harry smiled. Laura was always totally professional when they were at work together and even called him Dr Higgins.

'Would you like something to eat?'

'A biscuit will be fine,' he said as they walked arm-in-arm down the corridor. The lights were dim for the night and Laura's shoes squeaked on the polished lino floor.

Harry stood back as she preceded him into the kitchen. He followed her and closed the door. She held her arms open.

'Need a hug, Dr Higgins?'

'I do.'

Her face rested against his shoulder and Harry let the love for this woman fill his heart, giving him a measure of peace. He'd been so lucky to meet Laura. She'd given him a purpose in life again.

Harry knew not hearing anything from Charleville yet wasn't good. If the news had been good, it would've come through quickly. He glanced at his watch. Petie had been at the hospital down there now for over two hours, probably heading for two and a half. Harry went through the procedures in his mind. He would've had to get from the airport to the hospital, but that wasn't far and then they would've had to check him and then they would've had to get the radiographer in to do the MRI or CAT scan. Whatever they had decided to do.

'Stop it, Harry. I can feel you tensing up. There's nothing to be gained by thinking through it. There's nothing we can do from here. We can just be positive and hope and pray,' Laura said.

'I know, love. Problem is, I gave up on hope and prayer a long time ago.' He stepped back and slid his hands down Laura's arms. 'Come and have a cup of coffee with me, and then as soon as we hear anything and Matt gets off to Charleville, we'll go home to bed. God knows what tomorrow is going to bring. We need our sleep.'

Laura stood on her toes and brushed her lips across Harry's. 'One thing, anyway. Your patient in emergency is okay. Nothing a bit of antiseptic and some paracetamol can't fix.' Laura crossed over and filled the kettle and switched it on, and as she reached for the mugs, Harry's phone buzzed in his pocket.

He gestured to Laura and stepped out into the corridor where the noise of the boiling water wouldn't interfere with his hearing.

'Harry Higgins?' an unfamiliar voice said.

'Yes, Dr Harry Higgins here.'

'It's Ramesh Singh from Charleville Hospital.'

Harry swallowed. His mouth was dry. 'Yes, Ramesh?'

'Peter Cartwright is being moved to Brisbane to the Children's Hospital. He has a fractured skull and needs surgery as soon as we can get him there. The prognosis is not good, but Brisbane are preparing for surgery as soon as they land.'

'Is his father going with him?'

'Yes, they're flying out shortly. There is a team waiting for him in Brisbane.

'How long does it take to fly to Brisbane?'

'Under two hours.'

'So what do you think his chances are, Ramesh?' Harry asked. 'Your gut feeling.'

'He's critical, Harry, but he's holding his own. The longer he can do that, the better his chances are.'

'And how's Braden? His father?'

'He's bearing up okay.'

'Thank you. Keep in touch.'

Harry took a deep breath as he stepped back into the kitchen to call Callie.

Chapter 12

Bec left Matt and hurried home and had a quick shower. She pulled a face in the bathroom as she slipped her wedding finery over her head. The silk was stained with blood. There was no point trying to fix it, so she regretfully screwed the soft silk into a ball and threw it into the bathroom bin.

While she'd showered and packed an overnight bag, Sophie had filled her travel mug with coffee. Everything else she needed was down at Gran's house, and for the first time, she was grateful it was still vacant and she hadn't rented it.

An element of surprise lingered after Harry's request that she go to Charleville to support Matt, but she guessed he had Matt's welfare at heart and was making sure that there was someone for him. Someone who could sort out whatever he needed, like clean clothes. For a moment, Bec considered going to Matt's van, which she guessed was still parked at the Riley's house, to collect his mobile phone and charger, and personal things like his wallet.

No. She shook her head. That would be intrusive without him asking her to go. Even though they got on very well, they weren't so close that she had the right to go through his personal stuff.

Anything he needed she could go into town in Charleville tomorrow and buy for him. He could pay her back down the track; not that she was too worried about that. Despite Matt's itinerant lifestyle, she knew he was a good person and honest.

And how did she know that?

Bec shrugged as she closed the front door behind her.

I just do.

She travelled slowly down the Matilda Highway to Charleville, watching out for kangaroos as she drove, and it took less than an hour. Gran's house was on the east side of town opposite the racecourse. Partridge Street was in darkness when she turned into the driveway and went to the key holder under the electricity metre box to get the key.

Opening the front door, Bec tried to block the sad memories that always hit when she stepped into the house. Even though it was twelve months since Gran had passed away, the smell of her rose perfume had finally started to fade, and now there was only a slight hint of rose underlying a closed-up, musty smell.

Bec switched on the light and sighed. The living room seemed to have faded. It was no different to when Gran had lived there: the old-fashioned floral wallpaper, and the myriad of crocheted doilies and ornaments on every surface.

Gran had filled the house with life and laughter and you didn't notice the threadbare carpet, the tattered chairs and the peeling wallpaper.

Bec knew she had a decision to make.

Whether she was going to rent the house or sell it. When she finished her Master's degree in dementia she would move away, so it was probably more sensible to sell the place, but every time she'd gone to call the agent, something always stopped her. It just didn't seem right. It was her last link with Gran and she didn't want to let that go.

The way Gran's health had declined over the last four months of her life had been the catalyst for Bec taking up her Masters studies in dementia. She was determined to make a difference. Matt had looked at her quizzically when she'd told him that on their second night out. He'd asked her what she was studying and why.

'Dementia. I want to make a difference in lives.'

'Do you really believe one voice can make a difference?' he asked. It was the only time she'd heard cynicism in his voice. His conversation was usually witty and sparkled with dry humour.

His face was blank of expression, and when she nodded, he came out of the strange mood he'd fallen into.

With a self-deprecating chuckle, he'd nodded.

'You will be someone for me to admire. You're a much better person than me, Bec Hunter.'

When she went to leave the pub that night, Matt grabbed her hand.

When she'd looked down at their joined fingers, a strange feeling ran through her. A strong attraction that went deeper than anything she'd felt before.

'Come out for dinner with me tomorrow night? I'm not working.' He winked at her and Bec was lost.

Too fast, she told herself. She didn't have time for a relationship, even if that was what Matt wanted. She didn't make time to go out socially with any of her friends in Augathella, and here she was going out three nights in a row.

Matt Randall held an indescribable appeal for her so the next night she found herself in the bistro at the Augathella Pub being served by Sophie.

'What on earth are you doing working here, Soph?' she asked.

Sophie tucked the order pencil behind her ear and put her hands on her hips. 'Sean was desperate. He rang up and begged me to work two nights this week. He's had a procession of itinerant workers who only stay a week or two.' Sophie smiled. 'It all adds to the spending money for Fiji.' She regarded Bec with a smile. 'Can I ask *what on earth* you're doing out, Bec?' She turned to Matt. 'Matt, do you know that this is the woman who never goes anywhere because she's either working or studying? You must have charmed her.'

Matt grinned and Bec's face heated.

'I feel very honoured,' he said.

Despite the embarrassment, Bec thoroughly enjoyed that dinner out with Matt. Every time he held her eyes, a warm quiver ran down to her stomach. A quiver that she tried not to pay too much attention to; she had no time for that sort of relationship, and she decided when he went to pay the bill, that she would pull back on the number of times she would see him.

And now here she was after only a couple of weeks—and mind you, there had been six more nights out together in those two weeks—going to support him at the hospital. No wonder Reg thought Matt was more than a friend.

He is, a little voice told her.

He's *not*, she said back.

Maybe they did have some sort of a fledgling thing going and it appeared that not only Reg, but most of the wedding guests and Dr Higgins believed that they were in a relationship.

Once Matt was sorted, she'd pull back. Back to her work and study.

Matt Randall wasn't the person who could fit

into her life, no matter how much she was attracted to him. They put a value on different things in life.

With a sigh, Bec put her bag in the guest bedroom and left for the hospital.

Chapter 13

Callie

Callie jumped as her phone buzzed on the kitchen table. She stared at it, hesitant to put her hands out to pick it up.

'Sophie, it's Braden; can you answer it for me, please? I don't think I can talk to him. I feel a bit faint.' Her ears were buzzing and her head was spinning.

Sophie looked at Callie and raced around the table and pulled the chair back. 'Kent, pick up the phone. I'll look after Callie.' She pushed Callie's head down between her knees and crouched beside her chair.

'Are you going to be sick, Cal?'

'No, I just feel dizzy. I'll be okay in a minute. Just got to catch my breath.'

Sophie smoothed her hand on Callie's back. 'Take some deep breaths, sweetie, and keep your head down. Remember you've got to look after that baby.'

'Did I tell you?" Callie asked.

'I guessed.'

'I knew I didn't tell you. We were so happy. Braden was so happy, but I don't know if I can do this, Sophie. I don't know if I can look after a child. I didn't look after Petie.' Callie's breath hitched.

'Don't be silly. Take another deep breath and focus. Come back to me.'

Callie was aware of Kent speaking softly on her phone, but she couldn't listen. Her hands were shaking and she put them under her knees.

'Do you think we need to take you to the hospital?' Sophie asked.

Callie sensed how concerned Sophie was and gradually sat up. 'I'm okay. I'll be fine. It's just a shock of wanting to know what Braden is telling Kent. I couldn't hear it myself if Petie . . . if Petie's gone.'

'We have to be positive, sweetheart.' Sophie's voice was shaking too, and tears filled her eyes. 'We've got a stop being like this. We have to be positive. That's the only thing we can do to help Petie.'

'Are they okay?'

'They're both asleep. I'll go and check on them again in a minute.'

'Okay, mate, we'll get it organised.' Kent disconnected and put the phone back on the table. Sophie held his eye over the teacups.

'Petie is hanging in there.'

Sweet relief ran through Callie. 'Oh Soph, he's still with us.'

Sophie stood and put her hands on Callie's shoulders. Callie reached up and squeezed them.

'Tell me what Braden said, please, Kent. Was he upset that I didn't talk to him?'

'No, he totally understands, Callie. He said to tell you he loves you.'

Callie's breath hitched again. It wasn't like Braden to be so public with his emotions.

'He said to tell you both that they're flying Petie to Brisbane in a short while. The surgeons at the Children's Hospital are going to operate as soon as he arrives. He's got a fractured skull and they need to relieve the pressure on his brain as soon as possible.'

Callie knew she needed to dig deep for strength. She sat straight and focused on keeping calm. 'I need to be there with Braden.'

'You do,' Sophie said. 'Kent and I will get it organised. Callie, you need to get some rest first.'

'Do you need to take something to help you sleep?' Kent asked. 'Bec said there's a bottle of brandy in the dining room. Wouldn't hurt to have a couple of nips.'

Sophie shook her head and mouthed to Kent. 'I'll tell you later.'

'I'll get on the phone to Qantas and get a flight organised from Charleville to Brisbane. I'll cancel our seats on the eleven a.m. flight first so I know there'll be a seat for you.'

'Thank you, Kent. I'll give you my credit card.'

'No. We can sort all that later, Callie. Do you want us to keep the boys in town or take them out to the station?'

'I think they'd be better at home.' Callie turned to Sophie. 'What do you think?'

'I think out at the station would be best. Even though you and Braden won't be there, it will be more normal for them. We'll see how they are Monday. Maybe even take them to school for normality?'

'I trust you, Sophie. You know them so well. You'll be able to tell how they're coping. And they don't need to know all the details. Just that Petie's in hospital and getting looked after. Maybe when Petie's had his operation and he's on the mend you could bring them to Brisbane?'

'We'll sort that later,' Sophie said. 'Meanwhile, you need to get some sleep while we organise your flight.'

'I haven't got any clothes to take,' Callie said. 'And I'll need to get clothes for Braden too. I'll have to go out to *Kilcoy* now.'

Sophie put her hands firmly on Callie's shoulders. 'You are going to sleep now, and we'll get it all sorted for you. Come on, Cal. We'll find you a bed. I'll take you in and get you settled.'

Callie stood and Sophie put her arm around her. 'Feel okay? Not faint?'

'I'm okay now. Sophie?'
'Yes?'
'Will you stay with me until I go to sleep?'
'Of course, I will, sweetie.'

Chapter 14
Braden

The flight in the air ambulance from Charleville to Brisbane was one of the worst nights of Braden's life. He pulled a face as he sat in the waiting room outside Petie's room. It was right up there with the night that Julia had been killed in another bloody storm.

The flight from Charleville had to land at Roma after only fifteen minutes in the air because of the storm front that was passing towards the Darling Downs ahead.

Doctor Singh, who travelled with them, explained to Braden. 'We can't afford any turbulence, so even though I know it's frustrating for you, it's better for Petie that we sit on the ground and wait out the storm.' It was another two hours before they took off again, and then they were diverted north to Gympie to avoid the storm front as it headed east to Brisbane again. They waited on the ground for another hour and Braden thought that he was going to explode with frustration.

Petie didn't stir the whole time. The nurse sat beside the stretcher in the plane and didn't take her eyes off him. She took observations every fifteen minutes.

'His condition is stable,' Dr Singh reassured

Braden, 'but the sooner we get him to the hospital and into surgery, the better.'

Braden leaned forward and put his head in his hands. 'Tell me again what sort of fracture it is. I couldn't focus before.'

The doctor's voice was smooth as he answered. 'Braden, it's a depressed skull fracture and that's why we have to intervene surgically. With this sort of fracture, part of the skull actually sinks in from the trauma. Where that piece of roofing hit him has depressed his skull, and from the MRI scan we can see that it's pressing onto his brain.'

'And what are the chances of brain damage?' Braden asked.

'There will definitely be some internal bleeding and bruising, and swelling of his brain, so we need to get in there. That's what is causing his lack of consciousness.'

'But what sort of impact is it going to have on him?' Braden persisted as worry of the unknown clawed at him.

'It's too soon. We have to wait and watch,' Dr Singh said. 'Just take it in small steps at a time.'

The plane had taken off soon after from Gympie and they landed in Brisbane at 1:30 am. It has been a trip from hell. Petie was quickly moved to an ambulance and there was another car there to take Braden to the hospital. He looked down as he walked alone through the silent corridor towards the surgical unit. It was the first time he'd been away from Petie since the accident, and he felt as though a part of him was missing.

Braden sighed as he sat in the plastic chair outside the operating theatre. He was not a religious man, but he muttered under his breath. 'Please God, don't let him die. Please don't be cruel. He's only a little boy.'

##

Three hours later, Braden was still sitting in the waiting room. He jumped to his feet as a doctor in scrubs came into the waiting room.

'Mr Cartwright?'

'Yes. Is it done?'

'The surgery went well. We have relieved the pressure on Petie's brain and hopefully, there won't be any long-term effects. But it's a matter of time and waiting to see how much damage there is.'

'Can I see him? Is he awake yet?'

The doctor shook his head. 'No, he is still in a coma.'

Braden swallowed. 'What's the worst case scenario?'

'There's no point thinking about that yet, Mr Cartwright. Not until there is something to worry about. He is responding a little bit to stimuli which is a good sign, so we just have to be patient. I suggest you go home and get some sleep and come back mid-morning.'

Braden shook his head. 'I'm not leaving until he's awake.'

'Very well. He'll be taken up to a private ward when he is out of recovery. I'll ask one of the nurses to take you to the ward.'

'Thank you.' Braden held out his hand and the doctor shook it. 'Thank you for everything you've done.'

The doctor nodded briskly. 'Try to get some sleep. I'll see you later in the day.'

Once Braden was settled outside the private room in yet another plastic chair, while Petie was being settled in the private room, he dug in his pocket for his phone. Staring down at the screen, he swore. The bloody battery was completely flat and he hadn't given the lack of phone charger a thought.

There was a nurses' station about twenty metres up the corridor and he stood at the door of Petie's room. His little boy was lying in a large bed in the middle of the room. Both Petie's arms and his neck were hooked up to tubes and his head was swathed in bandages with a sort of cage around it. Machines beeped and figures that meant nothing to Braden flashed across the screens. He gagged as nausea hit his stomach.

This was real.

He stumbled up to the nurses' station and an older nurse with large glasses looked up at him. 'Mr Cartwright? Can I get you something?'

Braden nodded, but the words wouldn't come.

'Is there something you need? Something to eat or drink. I'm sorry, I was going to come and check with you but I've been on the phone.'

'No,' he finally managed to choke out. 'No, I don't need anything. I was just hoping that there was somewhere where I could charge my phone.'

'Of course.' The nurse opened the drawer beside the desk and pulled out a power pack with three different cables attached. One of these should fit it.'

'Yes, thank you. It's an iPhone. Thanks so much.'

'You go back and sit down there. I'll organise a cup of tea or coffee and some sandwiches for you. As soon as they have your son settled, you can go into the room with him. There's a comfortable chair in the corner. You look like you could do with some sleep.'

Braden nodded. 'Thank you.'

'I'll show you where the kitchenette is once I order some sandwiches for you. There's a twenty-four hour café downstairs. Do you have a preference for what you'd like?'

Braden couldn't remember how long it was

since he'd eaten; the last thing on his mind was food.

He shook his head. 'Anything will be fine. Thank you.'

Chapter 15
Jacinta and Ryder

'I'm sorry, love, it's not really the night for romance, is it?'

Jacinta rolled over and put a hand on Ryder's cheek as he lay beside her in the best room at the Augathella pub. 'It was the thought that counted. No one could have known what was going to happen this afternoon.'

She felt helpless. There was nothing they could do to help once the paramedics had taken Petie and Matt away. Ryder had helped pull down the marquee at the Riley's property. She'd felt useless and after a while had gone and sat in the car to get away from the dust-laden wind.

It was almost dark by the time Ryder came to the car. 'Will we go to the room at the pub?'

'Have you paid for it?'

Ryder nodded.

'Then yes. We're going to need some sleep. Who knows what will have to be done tomorrow.'

Jacinta jumped as her phone buzzed on the bedside table.

'It's Kent,' she said as she glanced at the caller ID on the phone as she picked it up. 'Kent? Is there news? What's happened? Is everything okay?'

Her brother's voice was quiet. 'It's okay, Jase,

no bad news.' The "yet" remained unspoken. 'I need to ask you a huge favour.'

'Anything,' she said. 'We both feel pretty useless here. Neither of us can sleep.'

'Sophie is going to stay here with Callie and the boys while I drive out to Kilcoy Station. Callie is flying to Brisbane tomorrow.'

'Petie's there now?'

'Yes, sorry. Braden called a while ago. Petie has a fractured skull and he's already in surgery.'

'And any prognosis yet?' Jacinta asked, her voice shaking.

'No, not yet, but Callie wants to get there as quickly as possible. Poor Braden is still in his dress clothes there by himself.'

'He must be going to pieces,' Jacinta said.

'Yeah. I was wondering whether you'd come out to the farm with me. I've got no idea what to pack for Callie and I wouldn't feel comfortable going through her drawers.'

'Of course, we'll both come. I'm sure Ryder will.'

Ryder nodded as she looked at him with her eyebrows raised in question.

'Do you want us to pick you up in our car?' Ryder asked.

Jacinta knew that Kent had left their four-wheel drive out at the station because they had been going to drive Sophie's hatchback to Charleville to catch their flight. 'Got more room for suitcases and things than Sophie's new hatchback.'

'The way things work out, hey,' Kent said. 'Callie will be on the flight that we were going to catch to Brisbane to pick up the flight to Fiji.'

Jacinta nodded. 'I knew you wouldn't go.'

'We couldn't,' Kent said. 'How could we possibly leave Callie and Braden to deal with this?'

'Okay, where are you now?'

'Sorry, I should have said. We're at Bec Hunter's place. Callie is actually asleep which is good. Sophie is sitting in there with her, and the boys were still asleep last time I checked on them.'

'Right, we'll be there in five. She's in Cavanagh Street near the hospital, isn't she?'

'Yeah, number twelve. See you soon, sis. And Jase?' he said. 'I love you.'

'Love you too, Kent. Something like this really brings it all home. We just live our lives, don't we? We need to care more about family and show everyone every minute of the day how much we care about them; you never know what's around the corner.'

***

It was well after midnight by the time Ryder swung into the driveway back at Bec's house to drop off Kent.

'Might as well leave the suitcases in the car because we'll be driving Callie down to Charleville tomorrow,' Ryder said.

Jacinta shook her head. 'We'll have to take Callie's bag in because she'll need a change of clothes for the flight in the morning.'

'I didn't think of that,' Ryder said.

'None of us are thinking straight.' Kent opened the car door and jumped down. 'Thanks for coming out with me.'

The porch light came on and Sophie came out the front door. She reached up and kissed Kent. 'I'm glad you're back safely. Has Braden called you again, Kent?'

'No. No more calls. What about here?'

'No, nothing yet. I don't know how long it would've taken to get him to get to the Children's Hospital. I imagine it's going to be the early hours before we hear anything.'

'At the absolute earliest,' Kent said.

Jacinta got out of the car and put her arms around Sophie. 'How are you, love? How's Callie?'

'She's still asleep. And I'm okay. I don't want to go to sleep in case the boys wake up. Even though they were worn out with all the running around they did at the wedding, they're both a bit restless. I just want to get that call that Petie's through surgery to have some good news for the boys when they wake up in the morning. Callie's been dozing on and off. She doesn't stay asleep long when she does drift off. She had a shower a little while ago, and we found some of Bec's clothes. I'm sure Bec won't mind.'

'Luckily we had our luggage in the hatchback ready to go away so Kent and I were able to get changed,' Sophie said.

'Your poor wedding dress, Soph,' Jacinta said. 'I wonder if the stains will come out.'

'That's the least of my worries today. I'll throw the bloody thing out. It's not a day that I want to remember.' She looked up at Kent. 'You know what I mean, don't you, love? It's a day I'll remember as our wedding day, but I think I'll forget the rest.'

Kent put his arms around Sophie. 'Just think, love, in a week or so this will all be behind us, Petie will be on the mend and on the way home, and we'll be heading off to Fiji. Then we can start celebrating our married life together.'

'Oh, I do hope you're right. I pray for that poor little boy. Life couldn't be so cruel, could it, Kent?'

Jacinta and Ryder said their farewells and when they reached the car, Jacinta looked back at Kent and Sophie, standing under the light of the porch. Her heart moved to her throat. They were putting on such a strong front.

Sophie put her arms up around her husband's

neck and rested her head on his shoulder.

This certainly wasn't the way a wedding night should end, Jacinta thought.

Chapter 16

Callie

Jacinta and Ryder arrived to pick Callie up at seven thirty to take her to Charleville to catch the eleven a.m. flight to Brisbane.

Sophie and Kent and the boys saw Callie off at the house. She was torn as she went into the boys' room after her shower. Neither of them had stirred. She sat on the side of Nigel's bed and looked down, his little sleeping face peaceful, his cheeks flushed pink, and his long eyelashes, the same as Braden's, fanned onto his cheek. He gave a little whimper in his sleep and rolled over. Callie tucked the blanket up around his shoulder before she turned to the bed Rory was in.

'Mummy,' he said.

'Good morning, sweetheart. Did you sleep well?' she asked Rory.

'I think I did. Where are we?' he said screwing his face up.

'We're at Aunty Bec's house, Rory. Aunty Sophie and Kent are going to take you . . .' Callie stumbled over the words. 'I mean Aunty Sophie and Uncle Kent are going to take you home today.'

'When will you and Daddy and Petie come home? Tomorrow?'

She saw the instant that he remembered what had happened. His little face fell and his lips quivered.

'Is Petie going to be all right, Mummy? Where is he? He's not with my other mum yet, is he?'

Callie blinked and firmed her voice. 'No, sweetie, he's still with Daddy at the hospital.'

'Can we go and see him after we have breakfast?'

Tears formed in Callie's eyes but she blinked them away. 'Sweetie, Petie's in the hospital and the doctors have operated on him to help him get better.'

'So he's gonna be all right?'

Callie couldn't answer truthfully because she hadn't heard anything from Braden yet. 'It's going to take a while for him to get better, but now Daddy and I are going to be with him, and Aunty Sophie and Uncle Kent are going to look after you at home. Can you help them with the chores, do you think? So everything's good when we come home?'

'We can do that. I'll make sure Nigel does as he's told.'

'You're a good boy, Rory. I love you.'

'We love you too, Mummy. We just want Petie better. Are you going to ring Daddy? Can I talk to him?'

Callie was reluctant to ring Braden, but if she

hadn't heard anything by the time they got to Charleville, she was going to.

'Daddy and Petie have gone to Brisbane on a plane. I came to say goodbye because I'm going to go to Brisbane to be with them.'

Rory's eyes were huge.

'You and Nigel will be okay with Aunty Sophie. And we'll ring you every day.'

Dear God, let them be good phone calls, with good news.

'I'm almost grown up now. And don't worry, I'll take care of Nigel. And Cottie too. She'll miss Petie so I'll give her extra cuddles and play time.'

'You're such a good boy, Rory. Give me a hug.'

Rory snuggled into her arms and Callie dropped a kiss on his hair. 'And I'll give you another one for you to give to Nigel. When he wakes up.' She dropped a kiss on the top of his head. 'Do you want to go back to sleep or do you want to come out and have some brekkie?'

'Some brekkie I think.'

He climbed out of bed and looked surprised to see he was still wearing his good clothes. Both boys had gone to sleep on the way home from Kimberley's house. Kent had carried them in and put them straight to bed. Sophie said Rory had woken briefly when she'd checked on them.

Kimberley had cleaned them up, washed the

blood off them, and fed them. They'd both gone to sleep as soon as the car had started, even though it had only been a five-minute drive.

'Wow, I forgot about the wedding. Aunty Sophie is still here? I thought they were going to an island?'

'They will be going, but not just yet; when everything's sorted out and everything is back to normal, they will go on their holiday then.'

Callie took his hand and glanced back at Nigel. He was still sound asleep. When they walked into the kitchen, Sophie and Kent were sitting at the table with Jacinta and Ryder, the inevitable pot of tea in the middle of the table. Rory ran across to Sophie and hugged her.

'Morning, terror,' she said. 'Where's your brother?'

'Still asleep.'

Callie turned to Jacinta. 'Thanks for dropping my suitcase off last night, Jase, I really appreciate it.' Callie had put on a pair of jeans and a T-shirt and pulled her hair back into a ponytail. 'I'm ready to go.'

'How did you sleep?' Jacinta asked.

'I got a little bit.'

'At least you've got a bit of colour back in your cheeks this morning. Are you ready for some brekky, Rory?'

'Pancakes?' was the hopeful reply.

'Pancakes I can do.' As she walked across to the pantry, Sophie spoke quietly to Callie. 'Have you heard anything from Braden yet?'

'No, but I'll ring you as soon as I hear or he might ring you as well.'

Callie declined any pancakes and had a quick cup of tea before she went back to the room she'd slept in and collected her bag. She took a few moments to compose herself as she tried to push the anxiety away. She had a road trip and a flight to endure before she reached Braden and Petie. She had to stay calm.

'Please thank Bec for giving us the use of her place when you see her,' she said when she went back to the kitchen.

The farewell was tearful, and Callie clung to Sophie. 'Take care of the boys. Don't let them do anything silly.'

'I'll be with them every minute of the day and night until you and Braden and Petie come home,' Sophie promised.

'Thank you.'

Kent put his arms around her and held her tightly. 'You take care of yourself too, Callie.'

She nodded. 'I know I really need to. I'll be sensible. I feel much calmer today.'

After one last hug for Rory, Callie climbed into

the back seat of Ryder's car. 'We'll see you all soon.' She blew a kiss as Ryder backed the car down the driveway.

Chapter 17

Sunday morning

Bec

'Hey? How's the patient?'

Bec stood in the doorway of the shared ward. Matt turned at the sound of her voice and the smile that spread across his face sent something warm shimmering to her heart.

'Bec! What are you doing down here in Charleville?' Matt reached for the bar above him and pulled himself up.

Bec had been standing there for a couple of minutes and had been taken aback by the sadness on his face. It didn't look like he was in pain; he just looked miserable.

Which she supposed was totally understandable. Her arms ached to hold him and make him smile.

She put a bright smile on her face and walked across to his bed. To her surprise, the other three beds in the ward were empty. 'Oh, I heard there was a guy down here who might need some company,' she said.

If it was possible, his smile got wider.

'Well you're a sight for sore eyes, that's for sure,' Matt said. His smile faded into a grimace as he looked down at his left shoulder. 'Or perhaps I should I say, a sore shoulder.'

'I called in last night, but you were still in recovery and they told me to come back this morning. Looks like you had the works.' She gestured to the tubes he was hooked up to and the big bandage around his arm and upper half of his torso.

'Yeah, I didn't get back to the ward until after midnight. I had a rough time coming out of the anaesthetic.'

'You look a good colour now. How's the pain level?'

'Bearable,' he said.

'On a one to ten scale?' she asked.

'The nurses have been asking me that every time they come in.'

Bec smiled. 'It's what we do. So?'

'A five. The damage to my shoulder wasn't as bad as they thought it might be. Minimal muscle damage. It was mainly a stitch-up job. I asked the doctor if he'd do it under a local.'

Bec raised her eyebrows. 'Silly boy.'

'I couldn't talk him out of it, but I really didn't want to go under. I think I got pretty nasty. They've stayed away from me pretty much this morning. They think I'm a difficult patient.'

'Matt Randall, difficult? I can't believe that,'

Bec said. 'They'll be busy. I saw a couple of ambulances lined up in emergency as I came in.'

Matt's face held a strange expression and Bec didn't probe.

'Well, you're in the best place.'

'I'm feeling no pain,' he said. 'I'm dosed up with something called—'

'Probably oxycodone in your drip.'

'Yep, that's what the nurse said.'

'Sleepy or dizzy?'

'A little bit tired. In fact, I reckon I could go home now.'

Bec shook her head.

'I don't think you'll be going home for at least three or four days, buddy.'

'What?' His eyes widened. 'I haven't seen the doctor yet, but I thought I'd be able to go as soon as they take me off the drip.'

'No, they'll keep you here for post-operative checks, and to manage the pain, if it was muscle surgery, and to make sure you don't get an infection, you'll probably be on a daily infusion of antibiotics. That was a pretty nasty piece of tin that sliced into you. Did they give you a tetanus shot?'

Matt shook his head. 'No, I was up-to-date with that. Had to get one before I could work on the cattle stations.' He gestured to the chair beside the bed. 'Sit down there and tell me what you're doing here. You said you came down last night?'

'I did. I came down here because you're in hospital and I thought you might like some company. Someone who can bring you some clean clothes, and anything else you might need.' Bec held his gaze for a moment. For a change, Matt looked disgruntled. 'I thought about going to your van and getting anything that you might need, but I thought that was a bit too . . . too friendly.'

'I wouldn't have minded but you wouldn't have got in. The keys were in my pocket.' He pointed to the metal drawers next to the bed. 'My clothes are in there. They need a wash.' He stared at her. 'I should've asked you straight up. How's that little boy?'

Bec wondered how much to tell him. 'Well, Mr Hero, thanks to you, Petie's alive. The doc said if you hadn't pushed him out of the way he probably wouldn't be here to tell the tale.'

'So, he's okay?' Matt asked.

'They've taken him to Brisbane for surgery to relieve some pressure on his brain, I believe.'

'Is he going to be okay though? Bec, be honest with me.'

'It's a matter of waiting.'

'Okay. I guess we can't ask for more than that.' Matt pointed to the chair again with his good arm. 'Please sit down, Bec. You look like you're going to take off, standing there, and I really appreciate the company.'

She walked around the end of the bed and put her handbag on the floor and sat in the vinyl chair that was on his right side away from the drip stand.

As soon as she sat down, Matt reached over and took her hand, and she looked at him. He wiggled the fingers.

'Have you got a problem with your hand too?' she asked with a smile.

'No, I just thought you might like to comfort me and hold my hand.'

'I don't think there's too much wrong with you at all, Matt Randall.'

'No, I'm feeling pretty good. I think you should go and find a doctor and tell him that. You can be my nurse and I can go home.'

'And sleep in the back of the van?' She pulled a stern face.

'Yeah, nothing wrong with that. I've been doing it for two years.'

Matt had never told her what he'd done before that, and Bec had sensed not to ask.

'Just be patient, Matt. Now, is there anything I can get for you? I'll take your clothes and wash them.'

'It's a long way for you to drive up and back just to bring me stuff and help me out.'

'It's fine, I'm staying in town. So what else do you need? Something to read? Some decent food? Whoops, I shouldn't have said that; I should be loyal to the health system.'

'Anything?' Matt said.

'Yes, I can even cook for you.'

'No There's no need to do that. I was thinking a cuddle would make me feel better. Or maybe you could even kiss me better?'

'Matt Randall, you're incorrigible.'

'It would probably help.' He still held her hand, and Bec ignored the little tremors that were firing in her nerve endings. Yes, she'd love to hug him and kiss him, but she wasn't going to.

'Perhaps some clean clothes or what about a mobile phone or something? Do you want to borrow mine? Is there anyone you need to call?'

She realised she said the wrong thing when his face closed.

'No, I don't need anything,' he said, not answering her question directly about letting somebody know.

There was silence for a moment, and it was a little bit awkward. Matt let go of her hand and ran his hand through his hair. Bec folded her arms.

'Sorry I'm a bit grouchy,' he finally said.

'You're entitled to be. And I'm a nurse. We're all used to grouchy patients. Are you quite sure there's nothing you want? Some grapes? Fruit? I can pick up some toiletries for you. What about TV? Do you want to rent that one?' She nodded to the television suspended in the corner. 'Do you have your wallet with you?'

'No, it's in the van.' Matt frowned. 'Listen, I will get you to take the keys with you.' He stopped and shook his head. 'No, don't worry about it because that means you've got to come back to Charleville. Forget I asked.'

'I'll give you some money and you can pay me back. I'm staying down here for a few days. I can probably stay here till you're discharged and I can run you back to Augathella.'

'What about work? Haven't you got to work?'

'Harry actually asked me to come down and look out for you. He's changed my shifts around so I'm not due back until later in the week. So I'm here to help you out any way I can.'

'He's a good bloke that doc.'

'He is.'

Matt put his head back on the pillow and closed his eyes.

'Pain?' she asked.

'No, I'm just enjoying that you're going to be visiting me until I get out of here.'

'Don't get the wrong idea, buddy. It's all professional.'

Matt's eyes opened and he held hers. 'Is it, Bec?'

Chapter 18

Callie

Sunday morning

The flight from Brisbane was an hour late arriving at Charleville due to the strong wind that was still blowing. Jacinta and Ryder waited with her but it was well after noon before Callie boarded the return flight to Brisbane.

Her thoughts were focused on Petie. Braden had rung when they were waiting at Charleville Airport.

'He's okay, so far, Cal,' Braden reassured her, and she sat down as a wave of relief broke through her. 'He's still in a coma, but the doctor said that's the body's way of letting his brain heal.'

But Callie could tell from Braden's voice that Petie was still in danger.

'I should be there with you about four o'clock, sweetie. The plane's a bit late, but I'll come straight to the hospital. Hang in there. Have you got somewhere to have a lie-down? Have you had any sleep?'

'No, I don't want to leave yet, not until he wakes up. I'd hate for him to wake up and have no one he knew with him. They brought me a comfortable chair for the waiting room, for when I can't be in there with him. I've been in and out of

110

his room. The medical team have been in with him most of the day, which worries me, Cal. The poor little mite is hooked up to so many machines and his little head is in a cage thing. It just breaks my heart.'

'He's in the best place, Braden. Just hang in there, I'll be with you soon. Tell me where you are in the hospital so I can get there quickly.'

Once Braden had given her the ward number and the instructions on how to get there, Callie hung up and had an emotional farewell with Jacinta and Ryder when her flight was called.

Jacinta hugged her tightly. 'Ryder and I are going to be in Brisbane in a few days, Callie. We'll come and see you. Have you got somewhere to stay there?'

'At the moment we'll probably stay close to the hospital. What about you? Where will you stay?'

'Probably a hotel in the city.'

'Look, I've got a huge house on the river. The tenants left it about a month ago and I just haven't gotten around to re-letting it with the wedding and work. You're most welcome to stay there. I'd say Braden and I'll end up staying there once Petie is out of danger.'

'If you're sure?' Ryder said. 'That would be wonderful, and we could help; we can ferry you back and forward to the hospital.'

'Keep in touch,' Jacinta said. 'And we'll let you know when we're on our way.'

'Of course, I will. They'll be lots of calls from Brisbane to Augathella over the next little while.'

Jacinta gave Callie one final hug before she boarded, and Callie realised how many close friends and family she had gained since she'd set off to Augathella.

'Just stay positive. He's made it through the op and is in the right place,' Jacinta said as Callie picked up her handbag. 'You go and be there with Braden. We'll go out to Kilcoy and make sure that Sophie and Kent are okay too. And the boys. If they need anything, we'll run it out.'

'Thank you, Jase. You're a great friend, love you.'

'Love you, too. Just stay well.'

After a quick hug with Ryder, Callie boarded the plane. Luckily she had one of the single seats on the left-hand side and no one spoke to her the whole way to Brisbane. She even managed to doze for a short time, despite the occasional turbulence, and then woke up when the captain's voice came over the PA advising the cabin crew to prepare for landing.

After disembarking, Callie focused on breathing evenly and tried to relax as she waited at the baggage carousel, planning what she'd do once she collected her luggage. She had two suitcases, and Sophie had made her promise she wouldn't carry them and would get a trolley.

The Children's Hospital was on the other side of the Brisbane River from Callie's house at Milton. It would be about a fifteen-minute drive so perhaps she would get the taxi driver to take her to the hospital, and then pay him to drop the luggage off at her house and take it around to the back veranda. Whether that was safe or not she would have to give some consideration and suss out the taxi driver that she got. She couldn't afford to have her luggage go missing.

Her fingers twitched, and her foot tapped as the carousel seemed to take ages to get started. She stood there, waiting for her signature red Louis Vuitton luggage to appear through the flaps.

The last time she'd used this luggage had been on the trip out to Kilcoy Station in her red sports car.

It seemed like a past life, although being back in Brisbane was familiar. Not knowing the country ways, she'd foolishly put her luggage in an irrigation channel, and it had been retrieved by Braden with minutes to spare before the water rushed down.

That was the first time they met, and it was hard to believe that just over a year later, she was married with three gorgeous little stepsons living on a huge property way west of Brisbane.

But Callie still knew her way around the city, so was confident in finding her way to the hospital. Her two bags appeared and as promised, she slid them onto a trolley and headed for the taxi rank.

'Callie!'

She swung around. 'Oh my God, Jen!'

Her best friend in Brisbane was running towards her.

'Jeez, Callie. I thought I'd missed you.'

Callie let go of the trolley and was folded in a huge hug. 'Oh, Jen. What are you doing here? How did you know that I was here? How did you know when to get me?'

'Sophie rang a couple of hours ago and told me you'd be arriving around lunchtime. We were down at the Gold Coast at a do for Damien's work so I left him there and bought the kids home because they've got a birthday party in Toowong late this afternoon.'

For the first time, Callie noticed the two children behind Jen. 'Oh my goodness, you pair. Look how you've grown.'

Callie crouched and gave Kirrily, her goddaughter, and Callen, her older brother, a quick hug. 'Hi guys, so good to see you.'

Standing, she took the trolley again. 'It's so

good to see you too Jen. It's been way too long. You promised and promised that you'd come out and visit, but you've never got there.'

'Sweetie, you try to get anywhere with two children. Anyway, talk to me as we walk to the car. Have you heard any news? Sophie was still waiting to hear another update when she called me.'

'Braden was going to call Sophie after he talked to me a couple of hours ago. He called me, just as I was about to board. Petie is holding his own, but Braden sounded exhausted.'

'Do you want to go to your place or straight to the hospital?'

'The hospital and I'll leave my luggage in your car, and catch up with you later.'

'I'll drop it at your place. Sophie said you were going there. No tenants?'

'No, they've not long moved out. I'll be looking for new ones.'

'Okay, I'm your chauffeur, your housekeeper, and your cook, cleaner, and whatever else you need, however long you're here.'

'Jen, you're an angel. You're just what I needed.' Callie fought the tears that wouldn't leave her. She wasn't going to break now just before she saw Braden.

'It's the least we can do.'

'I'll give you the keys to the house. Could you

take the bags and put them inside? I guess it would be sensible to stay there rather than in a hotel.'

'Yes, and Damien said you can have his car. We'll drop it over to the hospital when he gets home later so you can go home whenever you want.'

'You are too kind. I know you've got your hands full.'

'It's a different sort of busy as the kids get older though. And it's not that far from South Brisbane to Kangaroo Point. I can be there in a couple of minutes if you need anything.'

'Thank you, Jen. Having you here makes it so much easier. I feel like I've already got support.'

'Well, that's what you've got, love. However long it takes.'

***

Braden looked at his watch for at least the seventh time in the last half hour. He was waiting for Callie to ring to say that she landed safely, but his phone had remained silent.

She was upset, so she might have let it go flat as his phone had. The nurses on the ward had been great. They told him to keep the power pack in the waiting room as long as he needed it. Braden had lost count of the calls he'd taken since his phone had charged. There had been such an outpouring of love and support, he'd been overwhelmed. In the middle of the night, the doctor who'd travelled from Charleville had come to see how Braden was faring before he left for his next locum stint at Broken Hill.

Braden took his hand and shook it. 'Thanks, Ramesh. I appreciate everything you've done.'

'Your little boy is still alive, Braden, and his observations have settled, I believe.'

'But what about him still being out to it? The surgeon reckons that's not a worry. He's in there with him now.'

'That's correct. Even if he does regain consciousness today, they'll probably induce a coma just to give him that chance to be totally still and to heal quickly. Poor little fellow is going to be scared when he wakes up. He won't have a clue where he is or what's happening; that's why you're here. But make sure you leave and get some rest.'

'I will when my wife arrives. She should be here soon.'

'Good. You take care of each other. That is good that she will be here. Braden, you need to know, this could be a long time in hospital.'

'I know. I'm preparing for the worst.'

'There could be rehabilitation needed.'

Braden nodded, unable to speak without getting

emotional. He'd already considered various scenarios, and if the worst happened, they'd move to Brisbane, and he'd put Jon Ingram in charge of Kilcoy Station.

As Dr Singh turned to go into the room, the lift dinged up the corridor and sweet relief filled Braden as Callie stepped into the corridor.

Chapter 19

Monday morning

Matt

Matt closed his eyes as Bec left the ward. He'd been surprised when she walked in, but as usual, the delight of being in her company took over and he enjoyed every moment she was with him.

He still couldn't believe that she'd come down to Charleville to be with him, and he was even more surprised that Doctor Higgins had suggested it.

Perhaps she wouldn't have come if he hadn't sent her down.

But Matt knew he was kidding himself. He knew how he felt when he was in Bec's company, and he sensed that she reciprocated those feelings. He hoped she did, and then he prayed she didn't.

It would be too hard to go. And leave he must.

Bec had been in his head for the eight weeks since he'd first met her at that pub at Tambo. He still grinned when he remembered how she'd stayed with him instead of watching the male strippers.

When he closed his eyes these days, he could see her clear skin, her beautiful green eyes, her delicately arched eyebrows, and, most of all, the smile that lit up her face when she saw him.

The feel of her hair in his fingertips, and the feel

of her body pressed against his own on the two occasions that he'd held her close. They'd done nothing more; he was still to kiss her properly. Yeah, he'd brushed his lips across her cheeks a couple of times in a platonic greeting and she'd done the same thing, but Matt well knew they were both holding back.

And he knew he *must* hold back; this accident had been a huge wake-up telling him that he couldn't get too complacent. It was time to leave the district.

Being in the hospital was doing his head in, but at least it had made him see sense. He knew that it would be very easy to fall in love with Bec Hunter; in fact, glimmers of feeling were creeping into his heart every day, but he knew he couldn't, and he wasn't going to let what had begun as a harmless flirtation develop into a strong attraction.

Or more.

It was going to be hard to leave, but Matt had no choice; being in hospital had brought back all of the memories and the reason why he couldn't— wouldn't—love. He reminded himself that his heart was not whole, and it was never going to be given to anybody else, no matter how much it begged for it. No matter how much he wanted to, logic, his mind, and the dark emotions that lay inside of him assured him that it would not happen.

Matt had enough unhappiness and tragedy in his life, and he wasn't going to let that creep in again. He would not take the risk of losing anyone he cared about. He would not take the risk of having his heart broken. He would not take the risk of carrying the grief.

It had almost killed him five years ago and had taken a long time before he realised he couldn't stay in Cairns.

It didn't matter to him that he had a fabulous career, a beautiful home, a luxurious boat and a network of supportive friends.

The more time passed, the harder it got to be a part of that world, and Matt knew he had to cut ties completely.

As he travelled, he became a new Matt; he put on a brave and happy face. Everywhere he went people loved him, the jovial happy drifter, the guy who could sing.

God, if Marianne was here and could see him singing for a living, she would have died of embarrassment.

Bitterness filled his mouth.

Hey bro, she did die.

And it was your fault.

So just remember that, and don't go thinking that you can fall in love with Bec Hunter.

Matt wondered how he could get back to

Augathella and leave town without Bec having any idea he was going, but he knew it would be too hard. Maybe he could convince her to go back before he was discharged and he could get the ambulance back. Sometimes, the way she looked at him, he knew she thought he had no money. The happy-go-lucky drifter moving from pub to pub, station to station, job to job, and in a way, he'd learned to be genuinely happy.

The gnawing guilt that had accompanied him for the last two and a half years, that pervasive guilt that had governed his every action, his every feeling, and his every word, had all faded gradually as he travelled.

But, Matt told himself, he would never put himself in a position to go through that again. He didn't have the strength to begin yet again.

Saving Petie Cartwright's life—Bec had filled him in on the little boy's name and family background—had been a sort of redemption for him.

But no matter how many times he could do that or how many times he might be a guardian angel, Matt knew he had to stay aware of his past; it would not take away what he had done and that he had been the reason that Marianne had lost her life.

He didn't deserve to be happy.

He would move on, and start again in another

small town. It was time to go back to being the happy drifter.

Chapter 20

Thursday morning

Braden

Almost four days had passed since Petie's operation. Braden stood still at the side of the hospital bed, staring down at his youngest child. Not a flicker of movement, nothing apart from the ventilator that was helping him breathe. Not a movement of his little hand, nor the blink of an eyelid.

A tear escaped from Braden's eyes and he brushed it away angrily before he sat down next to the bed. He reached out and took Petie's hand and stroked his fingers with his rough hand. 'Come on, bub, wake up for Dad. Rory and Nigel are waiting for you to come home, and Apricot is crying for you, Aunty Sophie said. He misses you playing with him. Callie and I are here, ready to take you back to our farm. How good would that be, mate? I know you're enjoying this little sleep that you're having, and getting better every day, but it's time to wake up.' Braden's voice broke, and he pulled himself to task. He could not be weak.

He would be strong. He needed to be strong for Callie, and Rory and Nigel, and most of all for Petie when he woke up.

Maybe it was going to be tougher than anyone expected. Maybe he wouldn't be able to speak anymore. Maybe he wouldn't be able to run, maybe he wouldn't recognise them. Braden fought the thoughts angrily, trying hard not to let that second tear escape.

But whatever it took, whatever his son had become, whatever his son was, he would work with him, and they would get him back to the little Petie they knew and loved.

Being positive and having hope made all the difference. Callie told him that over and over, and he tried to believe that would somehow help.

The doctor said it could be days yet or even weeks. One lousy medico who'd appeared in the room yesterday had said it could be months, if indeed, he ever did wake up again.

Braden was not going to give up hope.

Callie was due to come in very soon and, for the first time, he was going to leave Petie's side. He squeezed his son's hand firmly. 'I'll only be gone for two or three hours, mate And I want you to know that I'm coming back.'

Callie was going to sit with Petie for the afternoon while Braden took a break and went to her house on the river.

She'd taken him through the map on her phone this morning before she left, and showed him it was quite a direct and easy drive, but Braden remained unconvinced. How the heck was he going to drive in the city traffic?

So much for the big, tough, rugged cattleman, who could take on a huge bull or a herd of steers; he was nervous about getting in a little car on the highway and encountering a bit more traffic than he was used to.

Braden lifted his head as footsteps sounded in the corridor, and he knew it was Callie.

She stood in the doorway, and her smile was gentle as she saw him holding Petie's hand.

'Going okay, sweetheart?' she asked.

'Yeah, I'm okay.'

'No change?' Callie looked across at the bed.

'No, but I was just telling myself he's sound asleep so he can get himself better.'

'Did the doctor come in while I was gone?'

Braden nodded. 'Yes, he was reassuring. He said we've just got to be patient. He said it could take time and I'm afraid you know me, that's one thing I haven't got. Patience.'

'I think you need to get out of here for a while, sweetie. I'll be fine here. I'll sit with him and you take your phone, but make sure it's charged. I've got mine; if there's any glimmer of him moving or responding, I'll ring you straight away. Just go for a couple of hours, find the house and let yourself in.

It's strange to know that you're going to my house for the first time and I'm not there.'

'Is it funny being back?'

'It is. I sort of feel like Callie Young again. When I'm there, I feel like I've been living a dream for the past year. And then I look down at my hand and see my engagement ring and wedding ring, and then I put my hand on my tummy, and I know that I'm Callie Cartwright. And Braden? I know just as strongly that Petie is going to get better. I know he's in there and I know he's trying to heal and we've just got to let him do it and believe he will wake up. Okay?'

Callie walked across to the bed and put her hand on Braden's arm. 'I want you to get yourself down to the car park, get out in the real world and face that traffic.' She smiled. 'Because I know you're hesitant about going out on the roads. Drive carefully. Take yourself to the house, and have a shower in a real bathroom.'

Braden had changed into the clean clothes Callie had brought to the hospital, and he'd been showering in a public shower amenity down the corridor.

'Make yourself something to eat in a real kitchen. Jen, God bless her, has been shopping and there's absolutely everything you can imagine in that fridge. Fresh fruit or you can heat some

Chinese, plus there's Lebanese and Mexican. Our lovely Jen really went overboard.'

'She's a good friend, and a good person,' Braden said.

'That she is. So, are you ready to go outside?'

Braden nodded slowly. 'I am. Don't you leave his side, will you, Cal?'

'No sweetheart, I won't. I'm refreshed. I've just been to the loo. And I'm feeling well, a little bit tired, but I had a bit of sleep before I came back. I want you to do the same. Across the road from the house is a lovely walk along the river. It'll do you good to walk along there. You've been cooped up here for days now, so go get yourself some fresh air. Have something to eat. Have a sleep, have a shower. Do some normal, everyday things. I'll be fine here. Okay?'

Braden put his arms around her and rested his forehead against his wife's. 'Have I told you today Callie Cartwright how much I love you?'

'No, I don't believe you have.'

'Okay, I love you. And I love that you're happy to stay here.'

'Why wouldn't I be? Petie is my little boy now. You've got to trust how much I love those boys, Braden. I love them the same as I'll love our new little one when he or she arrives. I can't wait to see Petie's face when we tell him he's going to have a little brother or sister and he'll know he's not the baby anymore.'

'God.' Braden rolled his eyes. 'Middle child syndrome. As long as he doesn't turn into another Nigel.'

'Don't be mean. We love Nigel.'

'I know we do,' Braden said, 'but God, he can be hard work sometimes.'

'He can, but I know you're talking to get out of leaving. You're wasting time.' Callie turned around and gently pushed him towards the door. 'This is my chair now. That corridor out there takes you downstairs to the car. Oh, did I tell you what sort of car it is to know what you're looking for?'

'No that would help.'

'Okay it's a bright yellow Captiva. Hang on, here's the keys. The number plate is on the key, and it's parked in the second row. When you come out of the lift, step straight outside that first doorway. Look ahead and you'll see a road with cars parked on either side. It's down the second road to the left. If you click the remote it will unlock for you. Now, get out of here, drive safely and I'll look after our boy.'

'Have you had lunch?' Braden asked.

'Go!' Callie said.

'Okay, okay I'm going.' He turned again and kissed her hard. 'It's two o'clock now. I'll be back by five.'

'No, you won't; that barely gives you time to do anything. You get back here by seven. That's plenty of time. Okay?'

'Yes, dear,' he said.

Braden knew Callie was smiling as he walked out of the room and ventured out into the wide world for the first time since he'd left the wedding.

There hadn't been enough smiles this week.

Chapter 21

Wednesday morning

Matt

Despite Matt's resolution that he'd be moving on, he still looked forward to the afternoons when Bec would arrive in the ward.

In the three days he'd been in the hospital, his pain had decreased, and the other beds had filled so that there were now four men in the ward.

A couple of them were real characters, and the third one reminded him of Old Reg from the pub at Augathella. He didn't miss a trick, but he was very quiet. He hadn't said a word yet.

The second afternoon when Bec walked into the ward, a big wolf whistle came from the far corner; old Jim Driscoll from out Morven way, who'd had shoulder surgery like Matt's was responsible.

Why don't I get visitors who look like that?' Jim said.

'Because you're a grumpy old codger. Be happy and sweet like me, and it's like honey,' Matt joked.

The fellow who reminded him of Reg smiled and gave Matt a thumbs up. Matt was starting to wonder if he could speak.

'Hey Bec, had a good morning?' Matt said with a wide smile.

'I have actually. I've taken advantage of the time here to start cleaning out my gran's house.'

Bec had told Matt yesterday afternoon where she was staying and how her Gran had lived there and she had spent a lot of time in Charleville with Gran when she was growing up.

'Mum and Dad used to travel a lot for his work and Gran minded me so I didn't miss high school. I miss her so much, Matt. It's because of Gran and how she was in those last few months that I decided to do my Masters in dementia.'

'Do you think that's what drives you to be so immersed?' Matt asked.

Bec turned him and raised her eyebrows. 'What do you mean? Immersed in what?'

'Well, from all accounts, all you do is work and study, and I do feel very special that you've taken the time out to come down here.'

'How do you know I'm not studying in the house after I knock off cleaning?'

Matt chuckled. 'You probably are, aren't you?'

'No, Matt, I'm not. My computer is still up in my house at Augathella and I have been totally spending the whole time I'm not here cleaning out the house.'

'Are you going to sell it?'

'I think I will. I think once I finish my degree, I'll be leaving Augathella anyway.'

'Where do you think you'll move to?' The thought of her moving anywhere bothered him.

'I don't know. I've got a good friend in Brisbane who said she can get me a job at a good facility, but I think it's a bit busy for me. I've got another friend up north. Someone I met through the course. He told me there are a lot of jobs up in Cairns in a couple of new aged care facilities that have opened up. Apparently one of them is at the cutting edge with the new dementia treatment. I was watching a program on one of the ABC shows the other night that talked about music and singing, and it aligns with one of the subjects that I've been doing in my course, so to find a facility that is actually implementing some of the things I've studied that seem to be successful would be very satisfying.'

'So, you're not going to change the world alone.'

Matt ignored the thought of Bec going to Cairns. If she did happen to move there, that would absolutely and totally be the end of them, because he was never going back there as long as he lived.

Bec sat down in the chair beside him, and a nurse came in and closed the curtains around Jim's bed. The other two men had their backs to them and were asleep. Bec lowered her gaze and looked down at her hands folded in her lap.

Matt frowned. 'Something's wrong, Bec, and I need to explain it to you, but I don't know that the hospital's the right place for it.'

'I'd like to talk too, Matt. Spending the last two or three afternoons with you has been hard.'

His spirits plummeted. 'Well, no one asked you to come and sit with me.'

'Don't be like that. Don't be negative. It doesn't suit you. What I'm saying is I like being here. I like being with you. Even visiting you in this hospital ward when you're hooked up to all sorts of things, I still enjoy being in your company and I want to come back. What I'm saying is I enjoy being with you way too much and it doesn't fit in with what I had planned for my life. Do you understand what I'm saying without getting cross or upset?'

He held her gaze thoughtfully for a minute before he answered.

'Yes, Bec. I do understand it because you just about said everything I've been thinking to myself.' After the last couple of days, he couldn't help himself. He reached out and held out his hand, and was pleased when she lifted hers, and her fingers curled around his.

'One and the same, Matt. We're the same, as much as we seem different.'

'Do you really think so? I don't. We're very different in our approach to life. I know that you want to make a difference. I know that you're totally focused on your job and your studies, but even though it's very different to what I am these days'— he saw her interest when he said "these days"—'even though we are very different, I know what you're saying. I enjoy your company and I know when I leave in the next week or two, I'm going to miss you very much, but Bec? I can tell you for sure, life goes on, and you'll soon forget about me and I'll forget about you.'

Her face was set and it was hard to read her expression as she stared at him, but her fingers remained curled around his.

'I don't like it but I'm going to go. I have to.'

'How are you going to drive with your shoulder like that? You can barely move in bed and feed yourself, so how will you drive a van or work anywhere? What are you going to do for money?' Her voice trembled with worry.

He shook his head. 'I'll be fine. I can camp out. Simple needs. Doesn't cost much.'

'And what happens if you get sick? What happens if you get an infection and faint when you're out in the middle of somewhere around a campfire with no one around you?'

'I guess I'd die,' he said holding her gaze and not letting any emotion cross his face.

'I don't want to think about you like that, Matt. I

worry about you and yes, I'm going to miss you *when* you go. And no, I will never forget you.'

'Never is a very long time,' he said. 'But you will, trust me. You will have to trust I can look after myself, because I'm a drifter, you know that. I move around with my guitar. I pick up jobs here and there.

'Why do you do that? Matt? How long have you done it for? All your life?'

Matt was torn. He cared about this woman, very much, and maybe she deserved the truth. Maybe if she knew the truth, she'd understand why he couldn't stay. Maybe she'd understand why he couldn't give her what he wanted to. Despite the fact that he admitted to himself he needed her, Matt knew he wouldn't let himself love her and he *would* leave her.

If it wasn't for his blasted shoulder, he'd disappear tonight.

It made him think of little Petie and it was an opportunity to change the subject.

'This is getting too heavy,' he said. 'Is there any Petie news?'

'No, he's still in a coma in Brisbane. Braden and Callie are down there with him. Now to get back to what we were discussing. Where are you going to go?'

'I don't know. I'll get to a road. I throw it out to

the universe, and I say left or right. Sometimes I go right, sometimes I go left. Sometimes I even have a choice of straight ahead.'

Her expression was tight. 'Speaking of straight, it would be nice if you were straight with me. I'd like to understand why are you drifting around like this. I'd like to know what makes up the real you. I sense that beneath this light-hearted drifter singer person there is something else, Matt. Will you be honest with me and tell me?'

Matt opened his mouth to speak. Bec deserved the truth, and he thought he could manage it.

Before he could answer, the doctor walked in through the main door.

'Hello, Mr Randall, time for me to have a look at that arm of yours.' The doctor raised his eyebrows. 'Well hello, Bec. I didn't know that you were here with Mr Randall.'

'It's Matt, please. Mr Randall is my father.'

'Okay, Matt. Bec and I go a long way back. Which hospital did we work at together? It's all a blur these days.'

'It wasn't that long ago, Roger,' Bec said. 'We were at Roma together for about two months.'

'The length of those back-to-back shifts made it feel like six months.'

Matt didn't like the jealousy that was creeping through him, but it made him realise how different they were. No matter how many words they put it into, there was no getting around the fact that they were.

Bec stood up. Her lips were pursed, and Matt knew that he'd given her a lot to think about.

'I'll go for a walk while Dr Gray examines you, Matt. I'll come back in an hour or so. Is there anything you need?

Matt grinned. 'Some more of those grapes would be good.'

'Consider it done. See you around, Roger.' He watched as Bec walked out of the room, her slim figure hugged by a pretty floral dress.

'Got it bad, mate,' the doctor said as he stood beside the bed.

'I think you're here for my shoulder, not my head.'

Chapter 22

Thursday

Braden

Before he went inside, Braden sat on the front veranda of Callie's home and looked across to the river. It was a very peaceful setting, and there were large trees scattered through the front garden. Lacy fronds hung off the branches making it a cool and private garden.

She'd obviously been lucky with the tenants. They'd looked after the garden and there were pockets of colour everywhere around the edges of the lush green lawn. It was a picture and Braden frowned.

How did Callie cope so well with the garden—or lack thereof—at Kilcoy Station? She didn't even have time to work on their back garden, even though Braden got a lawn going for them with regular watering from the bore. They often sat out there in the evenings at the outdoor setting Callie had purchased. But there was no colour, or any pretty flowers to look at. Callie kept herself so busy with the boys, plus working two to three days a week at the primary school, it left little time for anything else.

Braden vowed to himself when they got home

with Petie well again, he would get out in that garden and help Callie make it beautiful.

This garden was an oasis, and he hadn't even seen the back acre yet. He knew this house would be worth a fortune. A graceful old home on an acre opposite the Brisbane River between Toowong and Milton.

Braden took a final look before he walked up the steps and put the key into the front door. As soon as the door swung open and revealed a wide hallway, he could sense Callie. Even in the relatively short time she'd lived at Kilcoy Station, she'd put her mark on their home.

Braden could see Callie in this house: the same colours, cushions, similar prints and the same casual things scattered around. Candles, books, and the occasional unexpected colour, like the colour she had in the front garden of this place.

Again, Braden vowed to help Callie when they got home and he'd suggest maybe they'd get some new furniture and get the place repainted. He was so focused on the cattle and running the property that he'd never taken much interest in the home or yard, and to be honest, Julia had been the same. She'd been more interested in the horses, so they'd never turned the homestead into a home. It had been a house, simply where they lived, ate, and slept.

The boys deserved more. The boys deserved to

spend their lives in better surroundings.

On a whim, Braden pulled out his phone to call Sophie. He sat in a soft butter-coloured leather chair in the living room beside an old fireplace with a carved timber mantelpiece. There was even a basket of wood sitting next to it, even though it was coming into summer.

The phone answered on the first ring.

'Braden? Is there any news?' Sophie sounded breathless, as though she raced to the phone.

'No, love. Sorry to make you rush. I'm just ringing up to say hello and see how the boys are going. Maybe talk to them?'

'They're at school today, Braden. They were both keen to go, and I thought it would be good for them to get back. They went back yesterday. So there's no news on Petie at all? No progress?'

Braden shook his head. 'Unfortunately not, but the doctors keep telling us not to worry. But that's pretty damned hard when it's been this long.'

'I've been Googling,' Sophie said, 'and I can see where they're coming from. There are so many instances of people waking up from a coma, sometimes three or four months later. And with no . . . issues.'

'I think the longer it goes, the less chance there is of coming out of it. The medical team say they're really hoping he'll come out of it within seven to ten days. That will give him a chance to heal well. We can only hope and pray.'

'We are, believe me, Braden, the whole town is.'

'I was wondering whether you felt like a trip to Brisbane.'

'Yeah, of course we could. Why? What do you need? To help you and Callie at the hospital?'

'No. I was hoping you and Kent might come for a drive and bring the boys down. I've called Jon and I know he's doing a lot on *Kilcoy* now too as well as looking after your place while you and Kent were supposed to be away. I did ask Jon whether he could spread himself across the two properties. I hope I wasn't stepping out of line, but he assured me he can manage. He's got a couple of new station hands and Jim will come back to work if we need him too.'

'Oh, I can't see why not. I'm sure Kent would be happy to help.'

'It's not the helping. I want the boys to come down and you too, of course, Soph. I want you to see Callie's house. It's been a wake-up call for me. Seeing how she lived in Brisbane with her beautiful home and garden, and the lovely house that she created, I realise I haven't provided the right place for her to be happy in.'

'I think she seems pretty happy to me, Braden.

142

She adores you and the boys. I don't think it's got anything to do with the house or the yard or where you live.'

'You're probably right, but I'd still like them to see it. The other thing that we've got to consider too, and I haven't said anything to Callie, but I've been thinking if Petie does have a permanent disability, we might have to consider moving. I might have to think about selling the station or even putting Jon in as a permanent manager. I think we might have to think about moving to Brisbane.'

'Bray, do you think you're jumping the gun a bit there? Don't you think you should wait and see? It's been less than a week. Please don't talk like that. I know he's going to be okay.'

'I know Sophie, but it's hard. We have to be realistic and hope for the best, but also prepare for the worst. A number of scenarios have gone through my head in the last five days. I've had a lot of time to think sitting in that soulless room. It's sterile, and the only sound is the hum of the machines Petie's hooked up to. And I've had a lot of time to think about where my priorities have been, and now I know I need to spend more time with Callie and the boys. She told you there's a bub coming, didn't she?'

'Yes, she did and I'm really happy for you. I'm just so sorry that it was this week that you got that news.'

'It's a positive. It's a shining light at the end of the tunnel.'

'I wish I was there to give you a hug,' Sophie said.

'I wish you were here too. Talk to Kent. I still can't believe you're sitting there looking after the kids when you're supposed to be in Fiji and enjoying the happiest couple of weeks of your life.'

'The weeks with Kent are always happy for me, Bray. We don't have to be in Fiji or a fancy resort. In fact, I think we're probably happiest at home with family.'

'Well, I hope you can drive down here. Who knows, maybe by the time you get here, things might have improved and we can do some family stuff together.'

'I imagine even if Petie comes out of his coma, no, I imagine *when* Petie comes out of it that he might be in hospital for a while. I'm sure they'll have to run some tests and stuff.'

'There's plenty of room here at Callie's house. It's this massive old place on an acre with a hallway down the centre, beautiful timber polished floors and old leadlight windows. When I think about the red dirt on the windows at home. I honestly don't know how Callie puts up with it. I can't believe she's never told me about it. Maybe she didn't want me to realise I was offering her second best.'

'I told you not to be silly. You know exactly why Callie is living there. It's because she loves you and the boys. Look, I have to go, Bray. I was just heading out to go to town when the phone rang. I'll talk to Kent and we'll probably be able to leave tomorrow. What's today? I'm lost this week.'

'Wednesday.'

'Okay, so we'll get away either Thursday or Friday morning and we should be with you by Sunday.'

'Take it slow, and drive safe.'

'We will. Oh and while I think of it, Jacinta and Ryder are leaving for Brisbane in the morning too. Is there anything else you need to be brought down before we come?'

'No, we're right. They packed well for us the other night. I don't think there's anything else that we need.'

'Okay, I'll see Kent on the way out, and I'll tell the boys after school. I'm sure they'll be excited. Have they ever been to Brisbane?'

Braden shook his head. 'No.'

'Are you going to let them go to the hospital and see Petie if he's still in a coma?'

'I don't think so, what do you think?'

'Yeah, I agree with you. Wait till he's better and Braden . . . he *will* be better.'

'He will. Bye, Sophie. See you soon.'

Chapter 23

Matt

'Have you known Bec long?' the young doctor Bec had called Roger asked.

'Long enough,' Matt said.

'She's a good person. Don't hurt her, will you?'

Matt kept quiet.

'Okay, let's have a look at this shoulder of yours.'

The drips had come out today and they'd removed the cannula from his arm. Matt felt so free without all of those medical things hooked up to him.

His shoulder still hurt when he pulled himself up in bed, but he knew that he was getting stronger every day.

Roger peeled back the bandage, stared, and poked and prodded. Matt jumped a couple of times as the pain twanged.

'Healing very well,' the doctor said.

Matt jumped straight in. 'When can I get home?'

'Where is home? I see there's no address on your patient file.'

'It's because I live in my van and travel around.'

'Bit of an itinerant?'

Matt shrugged and then grimaced as pain ran

down his arm to his fingers.

'What sort of work do you do?'

Matt couldn't help himself. Maybe it was because this doctor looked so good in Bec's eyes. This guy was getting up his nose.

'I don't know what it is to you, doc, but I'm an accountant.'

'Just taking some time out, are you?'

'I am.'

'What does Bec think about that?'

'Bec is a friend and I really don't think that's any of your business.'

The doctor towered over the bed and folded his arms. 'It is actually non-negotiable because if you intend to go back to live in a van, I can't let you go.'

'What?'

Matt might as well not have spoken as the doctor continued. 'But if you're going to a house where it would be clean and you wouldn't be sharing public amenities, and you have access to a comfortable bed. If that was the case, I would be happy to discharge you in the morning. But if you're living in your van and using public amenities and out in the dust and the dirt, I'll have to keep you here for another five days or so until that laceration closes up. It'll need dressing every day, which means you're going have to come into the hospital here or at Augathella, wherever you're staying, and once the laceration has healed, we'll see about any future physio that you need to get that shoulder working properly again. It was a close call.'

'Shit,' Matt said.

The young doctor nodded. 'It is shit, mate, but I heard what you did and you did well. Sorry I got you riled before, but Bec's a good friend. She was lovely to work with and she's a very kind person. She's a very good person and I hate to see anyone using her for their own purposes.' He looked at Matt intently.

'I know she's a good person, doctor,' Matt said. 'And don't worry, I'm not using her. She's a friend, and I know she's a good person and no, I won't hurt her.'

The doctor patted Matt's good shoulder. 'I'm pleased to hear that. I'll see you later. I'll be back tomorrow morning. Think about what I said.'

***

Bec filled in an hour in town in Charleville before driving back to the big IGA on the corner on the road that led to the highway.

She parked in the car park and spent another twenty minutes wandering around and throwing a few groceries in a basket. She wondered what Matt was going to do when he was discharged because she certainly knew the doctors wouldn't let him go home to a van with no facilities. He had no clothes with him, but luckily the IGA had a small section for the basics in the absence of a menswear shop in town

If he went back to the van, there was no toilet, no bathroom, no shower. Bec realised she needed to call Harry to confirm she was back on shift on Friday afternoon. So if Matt was discharged today, she was going to suggest that he came back to Gran's house and have a couple of days rest, and then they could go back to Augathella before her shift on Friday.

He could spend some time at her house and if he was there, he wouldn't have to go to the hospital to have his dressings changed because she could do it at home.

She'd wait and see what the doctor said before she suggested anything to Matt. She was starting to see that he had a stubborn streak.

She refused to think about the conversation that she and Matt had had. She sensed something much deeper behind it and she was scared that he was just going to go to Augathella, get in his van and take off. Bec worried about his shoulder, she worried about his health, but more than anything, she worried about him disappearing from of her life.

As much as she was devoted to her studies and her job, the events of the weekend had made her rethink her focus. Braden and Callie were down in Brisbane with a critically ill child.

People, her friends, were more important to her than getting a high distinction in her next assignment, or taking that double shift when someone else was probably willing to do it.

She knew she had to rethink her outlook on life.

What if, by some strange remote chance, Matt said to her, 'Bec I really want to spend time with you, but I don't want to stay here. Would you come with me?'

What would she do?

Her heart told her what she wanted to do, and her mind told her, 'Don't be stupid. You've only known him for a few weeks. How could you throw away everything you've done to go away with a person that you know nothing about?'

Her heart knew that, even though she didn't know a lot about Matt, she knew he was a good person, and she knew that there was already a deep connection between them.

Maybe if he came to her house and stayed with her, they could explore that connection, and they could talk about what was going to happen in the future.

As she left IGA, she realised she'd forgotten the

grapes he's asked for, and she went back to the fruit and veggie section and selected a large bag of green grapes. It was the third bag she'd bought for Matt; he loved them.

Already in the short time she'd known him, she knew what food he liked to eat, she knew he loved his music, and she knew which bands he liked listening to, but apart from that, she knew very little about Matt Randall. The *real* Matt Randall,

Bec parked her car back in the hospital car park and as she crossed the pavement to the main building, Roger Gray walked through the entrance.

'Hey, Bec, your mate's ready to go home.'

'Yes, I thought he might be. Matt's healing up well and I know he's pretty restless being in bed. As soon as the drips came out this morning, he was up and walking around. When I arrived, the bed was empty. I wondered where he was; for a short while, I worried he'd been discharged.' She grinned. 'Then again, when I met his ward mates, it could've been the three blokes in the ward with him that made him go for a long walk.'

'Perhaps you're right.' Roger smiled back at her.

'So, am I breaching confidentiality if I ask what you told him?'

'Not at all, you're a nurse and an employee of the local health service. I've told him I can discharge him tomorrow morning if everything stays the same, but I've also told him if he's going back to live in a van, I'll keep him in for another five or six days.'

'He would've loved that,' Bec said.

Roger grinned. 'He did. I told him I hoped he had somewhere else to go tomorrow. Am I stepping out of line if I ask if there's a relationship there?'

'No, you're not, and no, there's not.'

'But you'd like there to be?'

'Roger, as you well know, I'm focused on my job and my Master's. How's Cathy and the kids?'

'They're good. Look, I'm sure you know we could do with the bed if Matt's discharged. Why don't you suggest that you take him back to your place, and you can change his dressings? For a week or so, and then he can come back and see me. Where are you working now? Augathella or Charleville?'

'I'm up in Augathella.'

'I thought you were,' Roger said. 'Well, if you're happy to have him at your place, I'll see him next week. If you could drive him down, that'd be great. I have to hurry anyway. I'm driving back to Chinchilla this afternoon. We live there now.'

'Say hello to Cathy from me.'

'I will.'

'See you around, mate.' Roger waved and took

off to the other side of the car park.

Bec made her way back into the hospital and along to Matt's ward. A television was blaring from the corner; from the bed of the man who didn't speak.

She put Matt's grapes on the cabinet beside his bed with her purse and keys. 'Maybe he's deaf,' she said.

Matt shrugged and his usual smile didn't appear.

'Bad news?' she asked. Bec didn't know whether to let on that she'd already talked to Roger in the car park.

'Not really. The doc said I can go home tomorrow.'

'Home?' she asked.

'Only if I've got somewhere to go,' he grumbled. 'So I guess I'm going to be in here another five days. Unless I stay at the pub. He won't let me go and live in the van. He said it's not hygienic. I have to have a bathroom and a shower and I have to come back to the hospital to get the dressing changed.'

'I'm glad you realise that.'

A grunt.

'I've got a suggestion,' she said.

'What sort of suggestion?'

'Well, why don't you come and stay at Gran's place; it's got four bedrooms. It's lovely sitting out the back in a private garden. If you want, that is. I don't have to be back at work in Augathella till Friday and it'll give you a couple of days to feel a bit better before we drive to Augathella. Then if you want, you can stay at my place for another three days. I'll drive your van back to my house, so you can have all your stuff, and as long as you stay with me, I can change your dressings and the like.'

Matt's eyes narrowed further. 'Have you been talking to the doctor?'

'Um, do you want the truth?'

He nodded.

'He was in the car park as I was coming in.'

'He's got no right to tell you anything about me.'

'Don't snap my head off, Matt. You're the one who doesn't tell anyone anything about you.'

'What did he tell you about me?'

'What would he know to tell me except how well your shoulder is healing? And that you're not going home unless you've got a house to go to and that was it. He was the one who suggested you stay with me, but you can go take a flying leap and stay in the hospital.' Bec reached to pick up her purse and keys. 'I guess I'll see you around somewhere.'

'Bec. Wait.' Matt seem to visibly relax and she wondered what else Roger knew that he hadn't mentioned. 'I'm sorry.'

'How sorry?' She paused before she reached the doorway. They had an audience now.

'I'm sorry for snapping your head off.'

'Okay, so what's it to be, Matt? Are you sorry enough to come to stay at Gran's house and then my place? Just remember after Friday I won't be around to bring you grapes and decent food. You'll be back on pre-packaged reheated rations. Nutritious but tasteless, I believe.'

He stared past her for a good two minutes before he spoke quietly. 'No ties, no commitment, and I come to your place.'

Bec's temper simmered again. 'Have I asked you for ties and commitments?'

'No, you haven't.'

'And I'm not bloody likely to.'

The other three heads in the ward were turning from one to the other as they spoke.

'Okay, in that case, I'll accept your kind offer. I'll come and stay with you here for a couple of nights and then we'll go and get my van and I'll park it in your yard. I can sleep in the van there and just use your bathroom.'

'I guess that's a fair compromise,' Bec said walking back to his bedside. She sat down on the chair and passed over the bag of grapes. 'Maybe these'll sweeten you up a bit.'

'Thank you.' Matt broke off a small bunch and

chewed thoughtfully. 'I'm very lucky I've got you here to look after me. I know I'm going to recover. I just hope that Braden and Callie are going to see the little fella recover.'

'Yes, we can only hope,' Bec replied.

Chapter 24

Braden stood in the doorway of the beautiful old kitchen. Polished pots hung from the ceiling on a rack and plants lined the sill of the leadlight windows. A plate stand with vintage china filled one wall.

He shook his head. He couldn't understand how it looked so good when there had been tenants in here, but he realised that they had simply looked after what Callie had placed here; she rented the house furnished. Pot plants, and all. He hoped that someone else would come in and look after it, because when, or *if,* they went back to Augathella, the place would be empty again.

When Braden opened the fridge, his eyes widened.

Callie had said that her friend, Jen, had looked after them.

She sure had; Braden had never seen so much fruit and food, or such a selection in a refrigerator.

It was like one of those fancy restaurants where you could get a choice of anything you wanted to eat.

Braden put three slices of pizza in a complicated microwave and then turned the coffee maker on. He stood there scratching his head for a minute before he figured out where to put the pod and how to froth the milk.

Every moment he was in the kitchen, doing something normal, he found himself relaxing a little bit more. Taking his pizza and cappuccino out to the veranda, Braden felt pretty chuffed with his efforts.

Of course, his mind was still with Petie in the hospital, but the tension in his body had eased considerably. Doing normal things in a non-hospital environment all helped.

A glimpse of the brown Brisbane river peeked through the lacy fronds of the poinciana trees, as he spotted a daybed at the corner of the veranda.

He kicked off his boots and stretched out; the last thing he was aware of was the muted hum of the traffic going past on the road along the river.

##

'Daddy, Daddy!'

Braden sat up disoriented, wondering where he was. He looked around and reality hit.

Petie had called him. He had heard his little boy's voice. He jumped up and pulled his boots on before racing into the house, knocking over his empty coffee cup on the way. He grabbed the keys off the hall stand, checked both doors were locked and raced for the car.

He would swear on his mother's grave that he hadn't dreamed of Petie's voice. It hadn't been a dream. Peter had been calling him.

Maybe it was the universe telling him that his little boy was coming out of his coma and damn it all, he hadn't been there.

The traffic was heavy as he went past South Bank and over the William Jolly bridge.

Finally, he parked at the hospital, and the parking fairy looked after him for once with a space right near the door where he needed to go in.

Braden locked the car and raced across the car park and pushed open the door; the lift was slow coming, and he tapped his foot impatiently. 'I'm coming, mate,' he whispered under his breath. 'I'm nearly there.'

He supposed he should have rung Callie to see what was happening, but if the medical staff were in there with her and with Petie, she would be focused on that.

He got out of the lift and tried to walk as sedately along the corridor as he could, but his steps were fast.

There was no sign of Callie in the waiting room, and Braden rushed to the door of Petie's ward.

He stood there in shock, his stomach churning and his throat closing.

***

Callie

Callie was aware of movement in the doorway. The magazine she'd been reading slid through her fingers and fell to the floor as she looked up. Braden stood there rigid, his eyes wide, and a shocked expression on his face. As she watched, his body seemed to crumple, and his shoulders sagged.

'Braden? What's wrong? Are the boys all right?'

She stood as he walked over to her, and her blood chilled as he put his arms around her and buried his face on her shoulder. She could feel his tears on her skin.

'Braden, tell me what's wrong. Please. You're scaring me.'

His voice was bleak and thick with unshed tears. 'Nothing is wrong; nothing apart from Petie, lying in a coma in that bed. I heard him talk to me. I heard him call my name, Callie. I was snoozing on the daybed on your veranda and I was sure he was coming out of a coma. He woke me up.'

'Oh no, darling. You were dreaming.' Callie reached up and wiped the tears from her husband's face when he lifted his head and looked at her.

'It wasn't a dream. I heard him. I broke every speed limit coming over here, and my heart was full of hope. And nothing's changed. His little eyes are still closed. His fingers are still on the coverlet and he's still hooked up to those bloody infernal machines. He's not going to make it, Callie. My little boy is going to die. I just know.' Braden barely made the chair as his knees went from under him.

Callie's heart broke as she gripped his shoulder.

'Calm down. Please calm yourself. It was just a dream. There's no change. His signs are the same, and when the doctor came in, he seemed a little bit upbeat. Petie's brainwave patterns have altered and he said that's a really good sign. I texted you. Maybe that's what woke you up.'

Braden lifted his head. 'What does that mean?'

'The doctor said the brain is amazingly resilient and it will repair itself through a process called . . . let me look it up. It's in my phone.' Callie pulled her phone out and opened the message she'd sent to Braden. 'It's called neuroplasticity. He said this is how survivors can make astounding recoveries.'

Braden visibly relaxed.

'I might go and find him in a while.'

'First of all, you stay there and hold his hand for a while. Let him feel your fingers. The doctor said even though he's asleep still, there is some sign that the brain is hearing and feeling. I think you need some contact with him. Let him hear and feel you.'

When Braden looked more settled, Callie stood. 'I'm sorry, darling, but I have to go. I'm busting to go to the loo.'

'You could've got a nurse to come and sit here with him while you went.'

'No, I promised I'd stay here and I did, but this little one,' she touched her stomach, 'is starting to put a bit of pressure on my bladder.'

Finally, she was pleased to see Braden smile.

'Well, hurry up, Cal, because when you get back I need to talk to you.'

She needed to go and didn't even have time to ask him what he wanted to talk to her about. Callie hurried along the corridor and stepped into the ladies' room.

This pregnancy business was very different to what she'd imagined. She hadn't realised the changes would occur in her body so quickly, even before she was starting to show.

As she washed her hands, she glanced in the mirror, and despite the worry of Petie, she couldn't believe how clear her skin was, and how pink her cheeks were. She didn't think she ever looked that healthy in her life, even when she'd been wearing all that makeup when she worked at the weather channel.

Wiping her hands on a piece of paper towel, she popped it in the bin, and then pushed the door open and walked back to the ward.

She pulled out the other chair and sat beside

Braden. 'Now what do you want to talk to me about.'

His smile had disappeared while she'd been gone, and he was sitting there leaning forward, his forehead wrinkled in a frown, his hands dangling between his knees and his head bowed.

When he looked up at her, she could see the traces of tears still on his cheeks, and her heart broke all over again.

'It's okay, Bray. We have to stay positive he's going to be okay, sweetheart.'

'I can't handle this waiting, Callie.'

'We're just going to have to. No matter how long it takes.'

'I know, and there are a lot of things we need to discuss. Going to your house this afternoon was a huge wake-up call for me. Why didn't you say anything to me?'

Callie frowned, not able to understand what Braden meant.

'About what?'

'About our house at *Kilcoy Station*.'

Her frown deepened and she took his hand, worrying about his state of mind. 'What about the house?'

'How can you handle it after living on the river there in that beautiful home?'

'I love living in our house on the station.'

'But it's nowhere near as elegant and beautiful as your house, and you look out over the river and have all the greenery, and trees, and your beautiful garden.'

'Braden, it's a house. It was my grandparents' house, and when I lived there after they passed and I was working at the weather channel, I wasn't happy.'

She had told him about her life when she worked in Brisbane, and when she'd been going out with Greg, that jerk sports reporter.

The only good thing that she'd had when she was in Brisbane were her couple of years of teaching and her close friendships with Jen and Christie and Nat.

'I couldn't live back here,' she said.

'Well, I've been thinking that we should move here.'

Callie's mouth dropped open from the shock of Braden's words.

'Move back here from Augathella? Why on earth would we do that?'

'Because it's nicer for you.'

'My God, Braden, don't you know the old saying? Home is where the heart is, and my heart is firmly entrenched in Augathella at *Kilcoy Station* with our family.'

'But what if we all moved here? Your heart

would be here.'

'And what would you do if we moved here? Run cattle in the backyard?'

He pulled a face at her sarcasm. 'I guess I'd sort of be like a fly-in fly-out worker and go out to the property some days and drive back here. There'd be lots more opportunities for the boys.' He glanced at Petie. 'And the medical care that Petie might need if—'

'So home for me,' Callie interrupted, 'would be where my heart is the times that you were here with us and it would be in Augathella when you went home.' She rarely swore but Braden had stirred her up. 'Please don't be offended, Braden, but you're talking absolute shit.'

This time, his eyes were the ones that widened and his mouth dropped open. 'What did you say, Callie? I've never heard you swear before!'

'You heard what I said. How can you even suggest that we move! We're not leaving Augathella and we're not moving back here to my house. We're not going to take the boys or me or you away from what we love. Our friends and our family. My job at the school. Braden, it would break my heart to move back here.'

Her husband's face was a picture. 'Really? You wouldn't rather live in Brisbane?'

'Yes, really. The only reason we would move

here is if Petie needed medical help, but have faith that's not going to happen. Plus we'd have nowhere to live. I've already talked to Jacinta and Ryan on the phone. While you were out, Jacinta rang me to see if we needed anything and she told me they're moving to Brisbane. I asked her whether she'd like to live in my place, but it's not *my* place. It's *our* place. I asked her if they'd like to live here. I think we need to keep the house for when the boys grow up and maybe when they come to university, it'll give them somewhere to stay. It's a house that was in my family for a long time and I'd be sad to see it go. I'd be more than happy for Jacinta and Ryan to rent it. What do you think about that?'

Braden nodded and his smile came back. 'What do I think about that? I think you're a very good businesswoman, Callie, and a very good friend, but most of all you're an amazing wife and mother.' He reached for Callie and she went to step into his arms.

'Daddy?'

Braden frowned and looked down at Callie and she returned his gaze. Neither was game to turn for a moment, but they slowly turned to face the bed. Callie knew she'd remember the look on Braden's face for the rest of her life.

'Daddy, I'm thirsty. Could I have a Coke, please?' Petie's voice was husky as he stared at

Braden. 'Daddy! Why are you crying? You're too big to cry.'

Chapter 25

Bec

Thursday

The drive home from the hospital back to Gran's house was interesting, to say the least.

'Nice day,' she said to Matt as they drove along past the water tower before they turned into Partridge Street.

His reply couldn't actually be classified as a grunt with a noise between a yes and a humph coming from the passenger seat.

'Feeling okay?' she asked, this time feeling a little annoyed. 'Matt, if you're going to be like that, I might have to retract the invitation and take you back to the hospital.'

'Like what?'

'Non-responsive and cranky.'

'Sorry, just give me some time. I'll be the model houseguest.'

'He speaks,' she said.

This time a glare followed the scowl.

'You know,' she said conversationally, 'it's quite nice to see the happy-go-lucky drifter does have a range of feelings.'

'Feelings?' he almost spat out.

'Yes, Matt. You're always so even and happy. It

wasn't normal. I don't know how anyone could be like that all the time.'

'Well, I've had time to have a bit of a think about what I'm doing. I suppose that's put me in a bit of a bad mood,' he said.

'Well, as long as you get out of it, we'll be fine.'

'How far away is the house?' he asked, looking like he was trying to show some interest.

'Just left at the next corner and along about a hundred metres. Gran's house is opposite the racecourse.'

'It's not a bad little town.'

'I like Charleville. It's got a lot going for it. A very active mayor and a responsive community. There's always lots happening for tourists, caravan parks, great coffee shops and lots of tourist stuff like the World War II base and the sky-watching centre.'

'Sounds like you'd like to work down here,' he said. 'Cairns would be very different to this.'

'Do you know Cairns, Matt?' It was good to have him finally talking, but she frowned when he didn't answer. He stared straight ahead, and when she glanced across she could almost see the wheels turning on his head.

'Yes, I lived there for a while,' he finally said.

'It's very different in the tropics to here.'

'It is,' he said.

'Which do you prefer?'

He turned his head and Bec took her eyes off the road for a second as she put on the indicator to turn into Gran's house. The look on Matt's face could only be described as anguish.

'I'm sorry, mate. I don't need to probe. Here we are, home.'

##

The first day in Gran's house with Matt was bearable.

Just.

They skirted around each other politely, and the easy camaraderie that had been between them seemed to have disappeared completely.

Bec knew what the problem was on her side, but there was no way she would ever let Matt know how she was feeling. He'd been in a hospital robe in the hospital, but when he'd come out after dinner wearing the PJs that she'd bought him at IGA, her mouth had dried.

How could a man look so sexy in a pair of blue and white checked short cotton PJs?

'I'd better go to the op shop and try and get you some clothes,' she said briskly.

His grin held a glimmer of the old Matt. 'Why? What's wrong with these?'

Bec pulled a face and went into the kitchen and wiped the clean benchtops again. It was because it was Matt, and that was the moment Bec realised how bad she had it. From now on she'd keep her distance, and find excuses to go outside, to be in a different room from him.

When she heard the television come on, she ventured back into the lounge room.

He looked at her for a long time as she stood in the doorway, and she let her imagination run rampant, kidding herself that the look on his face mirrored *her* feelings.

'I might go to bed now,' she said. 'Unless there's anything else you need? A cold drink? Another cup of tea?'

Matt continued to stare at her.

'What's wrong? Have I got tomato sauce on my face or something?'

'It's only half past seven. It's too early to go to bed.'

'Oh. I'd better watch some television then.' She knew her voice sounded nervous and she kicked herself for her crazy behaviour.

'And you can't go to bed yet, anyway.'

'Why not?"

'Don't you have to change the dressing tonight?'

'Oh, of course. Let's do it now before you get settled into a show. I'll go and get the dressing and the stuff I need.'

It was with relief that she left him and went down to the bathroom where she'd put the dressing packs the hospital had sent home with Matt. Scrubbing her hands for longer than she needed to, she dallied, and tried to talk sense to herself.

She just had to be professional, clean the wound, get the dressing on, and that was it.

Matt had gone into the dining room while she was in the bathroom and pulled a wooden chair into the room and put it next to the coffee table.

He was sitting in the chair looking like butter wouldn't melt in his mouth. Bec put the dressing pack on the table and stood close to him. He'd had a shower before dinner when he'd come out in those PJs, and all she could smell was fresh soap and man. His hair was still damp and curling on the edge of his neck.

'You need a haircut,' she said as she ran her fingers lightly over the dressing on his shoulder.

'Do I? Do you cut hair too?' he asked.

'No, I may be multiskilled, but I don't cut hair.' She gently probed the dressing on his shoulders. 'Is that still tender?'

'Only a little bit when I turn my head the other way.'

'Good. Are you ready? This might pull a little bit when I take it off. Take your top off.'

Bec pulled on disposable gloves and waited for

Matt to unbutton his pyjama shirt, and slip it off.

She closed her eyes briefly and held back the involuntary gasp as his bare tanned skin filled her vision. His back and arms were muscled, and the only thing that marred the view was the bandage. She had to resist running her fingers along the line of his neck where the cute curls touched his skin.

Gloves and all. Wake up to yourself, Bec chastised herself. She'd had many muscled and good looking stockmen in her care in the past and had never felt this.

'Right,' she said a little too briskly, lifting the corner of the dressing and pulling it. 'Excellent.'

It came away quickly and neatly without pulling at his skin.

'You've got a lighter touch than the nurses at the hospital.'

'I am a nurse, remember.'

'You're prettier than any of the nurses there.'

Bec's throat dried and she didn't answer as she placed the old dressing into a plastic bag, took off the gloves and put them in there too.

Was Matt flirting or just making conversation?

'I'm just going to wash my hands again. It looks good though. There's no redness and it's healing really well. You're a fast healer.' She scurried off to the bathroom, and washed her hands again, vowing that she would look at the wound and the stitches when she came back and *not* at Matt's tanned back.

As she walked back into the room, her mobile rang on the table beside her chair.

'I'll just grab that,' she said. 'You okay there?'

'I'm fine. Didn't feel a thing.'

'It's Jacinta,' she said as she looked at the screen. 'I hope everything's okay.'

'Maybe if you answered, you'd find out?'

Bec pulled a face at him. 'Hi, Jase. Everything okay?'

Jacinta sniffed and tried to talk, but her voice broke. 'Bec,' she managed. 'Oh, Bec.'

'Oh no. What's wrong?' Bec asked as worry curled in her stomach. She automatically walked over and stood close to Matt.

Jacinta's voice was muffled, and a moment later, Ryder came on the phone. 'Bec, it's Ryder. Don't panic. Jacinta's tears are happy ones. Petie's out of the coma.'

Bec squealed and grabbed Matt's good arm. 'Petie's okay,' she told him.

Matt stared up at her, and a huge grin spread across his face. 'That's fabulous news.'

'We haven't heard a lot of details. Braden rang Sophie—they were just packing to head to Brisbane. Sophie's calling everyone for them. As much as we know is that he's fine, and there doesn't appear to be any obvious issues from the brain injury. Sophie said she'll call when they get to Brisbane. Apparently the first thing Petie said was to ask Braden for a Coke.'

'Little pet,' Bec said. 'Oh Ryder, that's fabulous news. Give Jase a hug from me and tell her we'll be home on Friday.'

'We're heading to Brisbane on Saturday so we'll make sure we catch up with you both before we go.' Ryder ended the call and Bec looked down at Matt as she put the phone beside the dressing pack. Her other hand was still on his arm, and he'd lifted his hand and covered hers without her noticing.

His eyes shone as he looked up at her. 'Any more details?'

'Just that he's okay, and we'll hear more when Sophie and Kent and the boys get to Brisbane.' His hand was warm on hers.

Their eyes held and Bec realised the sheen in Matt's was from tears. She gave into temptation and put her other hand on his shoulder, and was surprised when he leaned forward and rested his head against her. She lifted her hand and smoothed his hair.

'It's okay, Matt. He's going to be okay.'

His arms went around her and he pulled her closer. Bec stood still as Matt held her.

'I worried that I hadn't done enough, if I'd been

a split second quicker, it would have missed him entirely.'

'And if you'd not got to him at all, the outcome would have been a lot worse for Petie. Let it go, Matt. You're healing, and Petie's on the mend, so it's time to move on.'

'I don't want to.'

Bec frowned and pulled back. As she did, Matt stood, his body sliding against her as he kept his arms around her.

'What do you mean? Do you need some counselling? I can—'

His chuckle was low and husky as he pressed his cheek against hers. He was so close she could feel the vibration in his chest against her breasts. 'No, I mean I want to stay in Augathella.'

'Stay?'

'Yes, stay. I don't want to leave you, Bec. I don't think I could.'

Happiness blossomed in Bec's chest as Matt's lips gently touched her cheek. 'I don't want you to leave either. I'd miss you.'

'Petie's accident, and seeing the community and friends rally around has been a huge wake-up call to me. I need to tell you about my past. I know you've had little respect for the drifter that you've seen me as. But despite that, knowing that you care about me, has made me realise that I still have some worth. I've been hard on myself for three years, Bec. There was an accident, and my girlfriend—Marianne—was killed in the crash. A drunk driver came through a red light, and I didn't see him coming because we'd been arguing. I was gripping the wheel and I accelerated through the light because I just wanted to get her out of the car and have some peace and quiet. Marianne was very needy, and now maybe I can see why. Maybe she knew her life was going to be short. When she wanted something she went for it, boots and all. She wanted us to get engaged and I wasn't ready. We were going out, but as far as I was concerned it wasn't serious.'

'Oh Matt, I'm sorry.'

'Let me finish. She lived for a couple of days but never regained consciousness. I didn't get a scratch. He came into the passenger side, and he wasn't hurt either.'

'It wasn't your fault.'

'But her family blamed me because I was driving. I'd been drinking but I was within the legal limit, but the story went around that I was drunk And the community turned on me. Our friends ostracised me and after a couple of months my guilt was overwhelming.'

'Your family?'

'I only have a brother and he lives in Perth.

We're not close.'

Bec's arms tightened around him. 'So how did you come to the west? I mean what happened?'

'I closed up my business, I bought my van, and I took off.'

'Your business?

'I'm a chartered accountant. I had many clients in Cairns.'

Bec was stunned. 'So the Matt Randall I've met is not the real you.'

'It's the real me now. I've found a side of myself that I like much more than the person I was. Money and things don't matter anymore.' He pulled a face. 'I've not been quite honest, Bec. Even though I drive my beat-up old van, and take pub work and "sing for my supper" as it seems, I don't need to. I've still got my investments, and I own a couple of blocks of units in Cairns.'

'Well,' Bec said.

'Well, what? Is that a good well or—'

'Just well. I'm processing this.'

Matt leaned back and held her gaze. His eyes held a look she'd never seen before.

'But more than anything, it's been you, Bec. You've unlocked something in me that's been frozen for three years.'

'And you've changed my determination to be a loner,' she admitted.

'If I stayed in Augathella, would you mind?'

'Stayed? For how long?'

'I was talking to Sean in the pub, and he mentioned he needed a new accountant. Apparently, most businesses use a firm in Charleville. I'm pretty sure I could set up a business and get some work. Lots of station owners struggle with their books.'

'You couldn't do that from your van though.' An unfamiliar shyness filled her and she forced it away. 'You'd need a base. I've got a spare room at my house.'

'For me to sleep in?' His mouth found its way back to her cheek, inching closer to her lips.

'No, for you to set up a workspace. I was hoping you might share my room.'

Pulling her gently against him, Matt's fingers slid up beneath her T-shirt and spread against her bare skin. Bec leaned into him with a happy sigh, her breasts pushing against his bare chest. She turned her head, so his lips finally touched hers. Matt groaned against her mouth and deepened the kiss.

She wanted, needed this man.

'You are the most beautiful woman I have ever known,' he murmured against her mouth. 'And I can't leave you, Bec. You're in my blood.'

A spark of mutual need passed between them and she could feel his heart pounding against his chest. She broke the kiss and lifted her head and smiled up at him. 'I think I need to finish that dressing, and then I think my patient needs to go to bed.'

'I think that's an excellent plan,' Matt said.

Chapter 26

Two weeks later
Callie

The day Braden and Callie Cartwright brought Petie home to Augathella was a joyous day that would be remembered for a long time.

Callie sighed as they turned into Main Street, and Braden slowed Sophie and Kent's Landcruiser as they passed Meat Ant park and approached IGA. 'It's so good to be home,' she said.

Braden glanced across at her. 'Almost there. Lunch first or groceries?'

They had some groceries to pick up before they headed out to *Kilcoy Station*. Braden had suggested that they have lunch at the pub; they'd left Chinchilla at eight and taken a break for the boys by the river at Mitchell.

'Lunch, I think. I've got a bit of frozen stuff to get at IGA. I didn't look in the back. Is Kent's camp fridge in there?'

'Yes, it is,' Braden answered. 'Okay, lunch first.'

Callie turned around and looked into the backseat and smiled. Nigel was asleep, Rory was playing on his iPad and Petie was looking out the window smiling.

'Okay there, boys?' She reached back and touched Nigel's leg. 'Nige, wake up. We're going to grab some lunch.'

Instantly awake at the mention of food, Nigel asked, 'Hot chips?'

'A hamburger first, and then we'll have an easy dinner tonight. I've got a mountain of washing to do.'

'And a red drink?' Petie asked as Callie turned back around to the front.

Braden smiled at her. 'A red drink for everyone.'

They'd been very careful not to single Petie out for special treatment during his recovery. After he'd regained consciousness in the Children's Hospital, he'd been subjected to a raft of tests and the doctor came in on the day he was to be discharged, shaking his head.

'Well, you're a miracle boy, Peter Cartwright,' he said.

Petie nodded and continued looking at Rory's iPad. Rory and Nigel had stayed by his bedside every visit to the hospital. The boys loved the house by the river where they'd stayed since Sophie and Kent had brought them to Brisbane two weeks ago.

The doctor walked across to the waiting room with Braden and Callie.

'Thank you, doctor. We owe you so much. The

care here has been amazing.' Braden shook the doctor's hand. 'And you're absolutely positive there's no brain damage? No long-term or later effects?'

'Every scan has come back clear. You'll find Petie might be a little bit tired when he gets back to his normal activities. The wound on his head is completely healed but could be a little bit tender for a while.'

'Should we keep him quiet?' Callie asked. 'I mean what about playing outside? Petie always goes nineteen to the dozen.'

'His body will tell him when to stop. For a couple of weeks after you get home maybe encourage more quiet activities. Maybe TV and computer games, and not a lot of strenuous play.'

'He'll love that,' Braden said.

Callie rolled her eyes. 'And so will the other pair. They won't have to be asked twice to keep him company if there's a screen involved. As they get older, they're losing interest in being outside if there's an iPad allowed instead.'

The doctor nodded. 'I know what you're saying. We've got an eight-year-old and we have to monitor screen time very carefully. I'll get you to make an appointment with my office for say three months from now. That will take us through to the beginning of January.'

'We might bring the boys down for a summer holiday and go to Sea World, Cal. What do you reckon?'

Callie nodded and smiled. Braden had promised they would be spending a lot more time doing things together as a family. Petie's accident had been such a shock, and it was still hard to believe he'd made such a fast recovery.

The main street of Augathella was busy, with visitors in town for the weekend. Braden parked on the corner opposite the pub. Old Reg was at his usual table on the footpath and he jumped to his feet, shuffling across the road to the car.

Braden climbed out and opened the back door for the boys. Reg's face almost cracked in the widest smile Callie had ever seen from him.

'Well, well, well, young man! How good is it to see you home?'

To Callie's surprise, Reg bent down and hugged Petie as he stood beside the vehicle.

'G'day Reg,' Braden said and held his hand out. 'Thanks for holding the fort in Augathella while we've been gone.'

Reg pumped Braden's hand firmly. 'All good here, Braden. You've got a lot of gossip to catch up on. A new romance in town,' he said with a secret smile. 'And another one on the way, if I'm right.'

'You're incorrigible, Reg,' Callie said.

The old man beamed as she kissed his cheek.

'I guess you're having lunch here at the pub,' he said.

'We are.'

'Anyone else coming? Being a Sunday almost everyone's free.'

Callie looked at Braden. 'What do you think? It would be a good opportunity to say thank you to everyone.'

'Sounds like a plan. Good idea, Reg,' Braden said. 'I'll make some calls.'

The word that the Cartwrights were back in town spread quickly and Sean, the chef at the bistro, had to call in a second waitress. The small family lunch turned into a long lunch with a large table of their friends celebrating Petie's recovery.

Harry and Laura were first to arrive and Doc Higgins crouched down and shook Petie's hand. Jacinta and Ryder, and Kimberley Riordan arrived together. They'd planned to have lunch together at Jacinta's place.

Callie was happy to see Matt and Bec arrive hand-in-hand. She nudged Braden and he smiled too. Fallon and Jon arrived at the same time, followed by Ben and Amelia.

'I think everyone's really pleased to see him home,' Callie said.

'I'm pleased to be home,' Braden said, putting

his arm around her shoulder as Bec and Matt came over to speak to them.

Bec hugged Petie.

'Welcome home, champ. Good to see you,' Matt said.

'How are you, Matt?' Braden asked as they shook hands. 'Arm's still in a sling, I see.'

'Almost healed. Bec's looking after me well.'

'We owe you big time,' Braden said. 'As soon as you're right to go back to work, I'll have a station hand position for you.'

'Thanks, Braden,' Matt looked at Bec and she nodded. 'But I'm taking up my old career again. If you know anyone who's looking for an accountant, I'm setting up an office in Bec's spare room.'

'You're an accountant?' Braden said.

'Yes, I had my own business before I set out on the road. Long story for over a beer one night.'

'Mate, I'll be talking to you for sure, and I know a few others who'll be looking for a new accountant. The firm we all use in Charleville is winding up. Jock Starr's retiring and he can't get anyone to take over.'

'Shame. I've noticed there are a few businesses closing locally. Here and in Charleville.'

'Well, you've come at the right time.'

Lunch was a happy affair, and turned into a very long lunch. Petie was given prime place at the head of the table with Rory and Nigel either side of him, and two jugs of their favourite fire engine drink.

Callie smiled as the pub got even busier, as Reg obviously told everyone Petie was home. Half of the town seemed to come to the bistro for lunch, and the bar was standing room only.

As soon as they'd eaten, the group moved out to the beer garden to make room inside for those waiting to eat. The lunch turned into an afternoon party.

Callie sent Braden to the car to get the iPad for Petie. 'He's not leaving my sight this afternoon,' she said.

Jacinta nodded as she and Kimberley Riordan stood next to Callie. 'We're off to fight the crowd at the bar. Would you like a drink, Callie?'

'Thank you. I'd love a lemonade. You can tell summer's not far off.'

She watched as the two women walked inside and thought what a pretty young woman Kimberley was. The school was so lucky to have her; she possessed a special caring quality that guided her every interaction, and not only with the children. Callie had noted if a teacher had an issue, Kimberley Riordan was always the first to notice and assist. Callie loved working with her, and was looking forward to going back to her part-time job at the school next week. She and Braden had discussed their plans, and Callie had decided that once the baby was born, she would stay at home for a couple of years.

Their lives were about to change again as their precious family grew.

Epilogue

Kimberley and Jacinta waited until there was a gap in the crowd at the bar. They squeezed in and waited their turn to be served.

'We'll miss you when you move to Brisbane, Jacinta,' Kimberley said.

'I hope you can pick up someone to replace me fairly quickly. Otherwise, it's going to be tight staff-wise.'

'Term four's not too bad with all the Christmas activities and end-of-year stuff. We'll be fine.'

Jacinta sent a glance to the end of the bar behind Kimberley. 'Quinn Calthorpe's not looking very happy these days. Weren't you pair an item once?'

Kimberly shook her head. 'No, just good mates. He was friends with my sister, Beth, at school, and he was part of the gang that spent a lot of time at our place when we were growing up.'

'I forgot you're local too,' Jacinta said. 'You were a few years behind me at school.'

Kimberley smiled. 'Not that much younger.'

'About time you got yourself a fella, honey. Romance seems to be in the Augathella air lately.'

Heat rose in Kimberley's face. 'No, not for me. I'm a career woman through and through. I'm aiming for Bob's job when he retires.'

'And you'd be the perfect person for it. Ah, here

comes Bill now. So bubbles for you or a wine?'

'I'll just have a soft drink too, thanks. I'm going to school after we have lunch.' Kimberley had bought the last round so she had only come over to help Jacinta carry the trays of drinks to the table. She took a step back as Jacinta gave the order to Bill, the long-time barman.

Quinn Calthorpe's deep voice filled the sudden lull in the conversations around them. When they'd walked into the bar, she'd noticed him sitting there, nursing a beer, looking unhappy.

As the noise picked up again, Kimberley stepped a little closer; Quinn sounded miserable.

It was out of character for Quinn to be like that. He'd always been the life and soul of the gang as they'd grown up. She hadn't seen much of him since his parents had passed away and he'd taken over *Merry Downs* station..

'Mate, I can't take any more,' he said. 'It's over. I'm done. I can't put any more energy into it. There's no money and this is it.'

Quinn listened as the person at the other end of the conversation obviously tried to talk to him. Kimberley turned slowly, trying not to intrude on his private conversation but the despair on Quinn's face as he pressed the phone to his ear stunned her.

'No mate, you're not going to change my mind. I'm checking out.'

Kimberley froze at his words.

Checking out. What the hell did he mean by that? Surely not what it sounded like?

Jacinta called over her shoulder. 'Here we go, Kim.'

Kimberley slid a sidelong glance at Quinn as she reached for the drink tray.

His head was down and as he stared into his beer he looked totally dejected.

Checking out?

Kimberley decided to forgo her visit to the school this afternoon, and catch up with Quinn Calthorpe. If he thought he was *checking out*, it wouldn't be on her watch.

UNTIL THE NEXT STORY...

Callie, Fallon, Sophie, Amelia, Laura, Jacinta's and Bec's stories continue in *Outback Hope* as we learn more about those who live in the district and those who come for a visit. Will the charms of Augathella keep them there? We say a temporary farewell to the Augathella girls in *Outback Hope*, but we'll come back for Christmas!

Coming in February 2023 - the final story in the Augathella Girls series

Who knew overhearing a private conversation would change her life forever?

When Kimberley Riordan realises how much trouble her long-time friend, Quinn Calthorpe is in, she knows she must find a way to help him.

But if Quinn discovers her plan, Kimberley knows he will leave Augathella and lose his cattle station. She enlists the help of her sisters, determined to make Quinn fall in love with her, even though she isn't in love with him.

But Cupid delivers unexpected results, and Kimberley's plans are destined for a fall.

What will she do when she discovers that Quinn has always been in love with her?

Outback Hope is available in:
eBook: books2read.com/u/3J659J
Print:
https://www.annieseaton.net/store.html

The Augathella Girls series.

Book 1: Outback Roads –The Nanny
Book 2: Outback Sky – The Pilot
Book 3: Outback Escape – The Sister
Book 4: Outback Winds – The Jillaroo
Book 5: Outback Dawn – The Visitor
Book 6: Outback Moonlight – The Rogue
Book 7: Outback Dust – The Drifter
Book 8: Outback Hope – The Farmer

OTHER BOOKS from ANNIE
Whitsunday Dawn
Undara
Osprey Reef
East of Alice

Porter Sisters Series
Kakadu Sunset
Daintree
Diamond Sky
Hidden Valley
Larapinta
Kakadu Dawn (June 2023)

Pentecost Island Series
Pippa
Eliza
Nell
Tamsin
Evie
Cherry
Odessa
Sienna
Tess
Isla
Also available in three boxed sets
Books 1-3
Books 4-6

Books 7-10

The Augathella Girls Series
Outback Roads
Outback Sky
Outback Escape
Outback Wind
Outback Dawn
Outback Moonlight
Outback Dust
Outback Hope

Sunshine Coast Series
Waiting for Ana
The Trouble with Jack
Healing His Heart
Sunshine Coast Boxed Set

The Richards Brothers Series
The Trouble with Paradise
Marry in Haste
Outback Sunrise
Richards Brothers Boxed Set

Bondi Beach Love Series
Beach House

OUTBACK DUST

Beach Music
Beach Walk
Beach Dreams
The House on the Hill

Second Chance Bay Series
Her Outback Playboy
Her Outback Protector
Her Outback Haven
Her Outback Paradise
The McDougalls of Second Chance Bay Boxed Set

Love Across Time Series
Come Back to Me
Follow Me
Finding Home
The Threads that Bind
Love Across Time 1-4 Boxed Set

Bindarra Creek
Worth the Wait
Full Circle
Secrets of River Cottage

Four Seasons Short and Sweet
Ten Days in Paradise
Follow the Sun

Others

Deadly Secrets
Adventures in Time
Silver Valley Witch
The Emerald Necklace
Christmas with the Boss
Her Christmas Star
An Aussie Christmas Duo (the two Christmas novellas)
A Clever Christmas
A Bindarra Creek Duo

About the Author

Annie lives in Australia, on the beautiful north coast of New South Wales. She sits in her writing chair and looks out over the tranquil Pacific Ocean.

She writes contemporary romance and loves telling stories that always have a happily ever after. She lives with her very own hero of many years and they share their home with Toby, the naughtiest dog in the universe, and Barney, the ragdoll puss, who hides when the four grandchildren come to visit.

Stay up to date with her latest releases at her website: http://www.annieseaton.net